ALICE *and the* DEVIL

A Ghost Story

STEVE GRIFFIN

Copyright Steve Griffin 2022

by Steve Griffin

FICTION

The Ghosts of Alice:

The Boy in the Burgundy Hood
The Girl in the Ivory Dress
Alice and the Devil

The Secret of the Tirthas:

The City of Light
The Book of Life
The Dreamer Falls
The Lady in the Moon Moth Mask
The Unknown Realms

POETRY

Up in the Air
The Things We Thought Were Beautiful

The Boy

1.

The boy with the toy sheep peeking out of his backpack stumbled on through the storm.

His yellow trainers splashed as he followed a black sand trail through the heather. Rain pummelled the top of his waterproof hood. The wind made his fingers raw. He thought about poor Sheepy being soaked, but there was nothing he could do about it now.

The trail veered away downhill. He stopped and stared at the farm it descended to, down in the valley below. He saw the large, granite-looking block of the farmhouse, the rickety barns and outhouses, the vegetable plot. He didn't like it, but it took a while before he realised why. It was that single-story wooden building nearest him, a short distance from the others, with its two large, black entrances side by side. No doors. Just the giant, perfectly square openings. Gaping at him. Like eyes. Like the eyes of the farm staring at him.

The boy grimaced and shuddered in the cold wind, in the cold rain, then trudged on, following a narrower path through the heather, trying not to look again at the farm.

'Nearly there, Sheepy,' he said, trying to reassure himself. Sheepy continued to look back the way the boy had come, his two small, stitched black eyes friendly enough but somewhat bedraggled, a little more uncertain or fearful than usual, his long ears sopping with rain.

Overhead the clouds were as dense as they could get, deep mauve-grey, making dark of the day. White light flashed in the valley and moments later the air shuddered with thunder. The boy's shoes splashed mud. He refused himself permission to glance back over his shoulder at the black holes of the barn. On the left, the thorny, gnarled limbs of a hawthorn shook at him, reminding him of the Grackle. He walked faster.

The boy's pink cheeks were wet but not with tears, with the rain, which he could feel soaking through his thin jacket. It wasn't properly waterproof, he knew that, but what could he do? He needed to reach the house.

 At one stage his foot slipped on a stone and his ankle twisted sharply, causing him to wince with pain. He stopped, reaching down to press at his ankle with both hands. His fingers were ice cold and white. Thankfully, the ache passed quickly and he was able to walk on, in between the pink of the hunkered heather.

'Oh my,' he said to himself, the first time he'd ever used the expression. It was something his grandad said to himself occasionally. Oh my what? God?

A ridge came up, a few large grey stones broken through a patch of bracken like whales breaching in the storm. The boy navigated a path through their slick wetness, wary, and when they finished he half-jogged, half-slid down a small slope. Then, a short distance up the hillside, he spotted it.

The house. The Right House.

A white two-storey stone cottage with a tiled roof and small drystone-walled garden, reached by an access road that came up the far side of the hill.

Taking a deep breath – he was very nervous – the boy left the sheep trail and picked his way through the awkward brush towards the house.

2.

It wasn't the best thing she'd ever written, but it would have to do.

Alice Deaton typed *Here you go, Dave, just in time!* on the email, attached the funding bid, and, after a brief check, hit send. Even though it was a pretty lacklustre document, she still felt a small frisson of joy at being released from this burden she had been struggling with for several weeks. Improving her case sentence by sentence. Hoping for an arrangement of words that would pluck heartstrings to release cash. What a job. But someone had to do it if there was any hope of bringing Farthingbridge House, the beautiful Victorian manor partially destroyed by fire, back to its former glory.

At least her boss, Victor, had found this fundraising job for her to do, with the house's continued closure. She couldn't go back to her old post as visitor manager. And – icing on the cake – he'd offered her his second home in the Peak District from which to do it. He'd wanted a house sitter to look after the place as it had been empty for too long, and there was no problem for her to work remotely with the fundraising team.

Initially, she'd been concerned about the fact it was so isolated, after all that had happened in Wales at Peacehaven with Susannah, Eloise, and Jo… What if the thoughts, the guilt, that had plagued her for months were to boil up again in the remote setting? Without any real company, the balancing presence of others, might her own mind collapse in on itself? Might the isolation send her over the edge?

But in the end she had gambled it would do her more good than harm. She was an introvert by nature, and the calm and distance might help her process things.

And so far, she had been right. She was feeling better. The healing wasn't complete – probably never would be – but it was getting there.

At the sound of sustained rattling, she looked out at the weather. The wind was violent, blasting rain sideways at the windowpanes, splattering them with mercurial silver. Beyond, dark clouds bore oppressively across the moors. There was a rumble and a flash of lightning.

How long was this rainstorm going to last? she wondered. It had started halfway through the morning and was still going strong.

Alice stood and felt a stiffness on the top of her thighs. She was walking a lot up here, loving the big open spaces, but she was sitting a lot too, the work endless hours in front of a screen. She kept noticing a numbness in the back of her legs that was concerning.

Stretching her lower back, she went away from the kitchen table where she worked and clicked on the kettle.

And then, amidst the hum of the rain, spotted the boy.

3.

He was struggling with the gate, hunched up like he was under attack. On his back was a small blue pack out of which sprawled an animal, no, a cuddly toy. The boy's anorak was soaked through, pale green under the arms but dark olive everywhere else.

Alice shivered, felt a moment of anxiety. What was he doing out there?

She shoved her feet into her boots by the back door and without bothering to lace them flung the door open and stumbled outside.

'Hey – are you OK?' she called.

He didn't hear her, the rain was so loud. He was still trying to budge the metal latch. Alice hurried down to the gate, saw him straighten in shock as she reached down and did it for him.

He looked at her in bewilderment, her hair lank with rain.

'Come inside!' she shouted.

He followed her in.

4.

'What were you doing out there?' she said, as she slammed the door behind him.

He looked up at her, lips dipped at the edges. He had a thin face, pale but blushed with the cold. His eyes were brown with long dark lashes. Alice thought he looked very uncertain and wondered if he was about to cry.

'Let me get you a warm drink,' she said. 'Where's your mum and dad?'

'They're dead,' he said, as he twisted and tugged off his drenched backpack. He pulled the toy, a very wet, cream coloured sheep, out of the pack.

'Oh,' said Alice, watching him examine the sheep.

'Sheepy's wet,' he said.

9

'Let me… I'll put him on the radiator. He'll dry off,' said Alice.

He stared at her outstretched hand before passing her the sheep.

Alice tucked it carefully on top of the radiator. She flicked on the kettle again. 'Take off your coat and I'll get you a towel,' she said.

The boy remained stock still but gave a small nod. Alice hurried into the utility room and pulled one of the towels from the dryer. It was still warm. When she got back the boy was standing there in his sopping coat.

'Take it off,' she said, setting the towel down on a seat beside him. 'Do you want some hot chocolate?'

'Yes. Yes please.'

She heaped two large spoonfuls into a mug and poured the hot water on, noticing he was slowly removing his waterproof jacket. When he'd finished he picked up the towel and began to rub his hair.

'You're not alone?' she said, looking out across the increasingly shadowed moor. It was past four, it would be dark soon. 'Are you lost? Who were you with?'

He stopped rubbing and shook his head. 'No one,' he said.

'Where's home? Were you playing on the moors?'

'The Rectory,' he said, as if she'd know it.

'Where's that?'

'Over the other side of the mountain. Near Tiss.'

She suppressed a smile. It was sweet he thought of it as a mountain. 'Yes, Tiss, that's the village in the next valley, isn't it?' She hadn't been there but she'd seen it on a map when she was hiking.

He nodded.

'Do you – who do you live with if your parents are… no longer alive?'

'My grandad.'

'Does he know you're out?'

She passed him the chocolate and he took a sip and grimaced.

'Careful, it's hot!' she said.

He continued to look closely at the spinning froth, his desire to drink the delicious liquid fighting his fear of getting burnt.

'Does your grandad know you're out?' she asked again.

The boy shook his head.

'Don't you think we'd better let him know? Do you have his number, I can give him a call? Perhaps he can come and collect you. You don't want to be walking back in this weather.'

The boy looked up at her and said:

'I don't want him to come here. I want you to come home with me.'

Alice laughed, surprised at his tone. Precise – almost arrogant, demanding. Not like a boy at all. 'Well,' she said. 'I suppose I could. But it might be better for him to come here because, if you look outside, you'll see I haven't got a car. That's my scooter poking out the shed there, and I don't have another helmet.'

'We'll have to walk then.'

She snorted. 'We will?'

'Yes.'

'Look at the rain. Tiss is two or three miles away. I think you're going to have to call your grandad…' She had a sudden worry. What if the boy had run away from home for some reason?

'No. Grandad is ill in bed. He's been doing all he can. But he's too poorly to drive. So we'll have to walk back, as you don't have a car.'

Alice looked at him, thinking she'd never seen a boy of his age – nine or ten – quite so self-assured. And then she saw his lips wobble and realised he was on the verge of tears. He was overcompensating. She wanted to hug him but thought she'd better not.

And then, as his tears welled, she did.

5.

As soon as she put her arms around him, he began to shudder and sniff. Alice rubbed his back and stroked his damp hair.

'You're alright,' she said. 'You're safe here. What's the problem?'

He was quiet for a moment, silently sobbing, and then he said: 'I don't know what to do…'

'Is it your grandad? His health? How is he?' she asked.

His chest jerked with two sharp breaths.

'Does he need help urgently? It might be best to call an ambulance.'

A pause. 'No.'

'Maybe the police…?'

'No.'

'They might be the right ones to call.'

'No.'

She felt him relax slightly, eased him back with her hands to look at his face. 'You sound very sure,' she said.

'I am.'

'So only I will do?' she said lightly, half joking.

'Yes,' he replied, looking her in the eye. Then looking down at the polished tiled floor.

Alice had the strange feeling again. Anxiety. Uncanniness.

'Why?' she said.

'Because she told me to come and get you. To come here. To the Right House.'

'Who told you that?'

'Her. The Grackle.'

'The Grackle. That's a funny name. Who's the Grackle?'

The boy looked across at his sheep, now steaming on the hot radiator. Then he looked back at the table where Alice had set down his drink. He picked it up, took the tiniest two sips, then sat down on a chair.

'She's a scary lady with a horrible face who comes to me in the night.'

'Oh,' said Alice. The boy's appearance in the storm was strange, but she was realising that might only be the start of it. She felt the flurry of nerves in her gut and took a deep breath.

'Is the Grackle real or do you think she might be… imaginary?'

The boy looked at her and said calmly. 'She's a ghost.'

Alice glanced out the window at the rain.

'Are you sure?'

Suddenly, the boy laughed. 'I knew it!' he said. 'She was right. You *are* one of the ones who can see, aren't you?'

Alice began to pour herself some coffee, not meeting his gaze. Then she stopped, the smell too rich, making her feel quite sick.

'Yes,' she said quietly. 'I can see ghosts.'

'And that's why she told me to come here. Because you can help us. You can help Grandad and me. You can help us defeat him!'

'Defeat who?'

'Him.' The boy beamed, almost manically. 'The Devil.'

6.

'We'll call the police.'

There was no way she could handle this right now. Not after Wales. She reached across the breakfast counter and picked up her phone.

'The police can't do a thing!'

'How do you know?'

'Last I heard, they didn't have a Paranormal department.'

She stared at him, surprised by his sarcasm. Despite the facile tone, the vulnerability remained in his eyes.

'I can't help you,' she said.

'But you just said, you see them!'

'That might be so,' said Alice. 'But I can't help you.'

'Why not? You could be the only one who can!'

'Because…' What could she tell him? What would a young boy understand? 'Because I've had problems with spirits, recently. I am still recovering from those problems.'

The boy wrinkled his nose, but not antagonistically. Painfully. He was in pain. He stared down at the kitchen floor and didn't say anything. Alice could feel the responsibility building in the silence, like she was underwater, being trapped down by rocks.

'I can't do it,' she said quietly.

'Fine!' he stood up, the chair scraping Victor's immaculate floor. He turned around and began to march back towards the door.

'What are you doing?' she said.

'Going home.'

'Let me call the police.'

'I told you, they won't help!'

He picked up his damp pack, snatched the sheep off the radiator. He shoved it into the pack, where it resumed its resigned slouch over the top.

'No,' she said, as he hoisted the bag on his back and grabbed the door handle.

He looked round at her.

'Wait,' she said, simply.

7.

She left him in the kitchen while she went upstairs to throw a few things in a pack.

Her mind was a storm of confusion, echoing the rain outside. She thought about Susannah's email last year, asking her to come to the guest house, Peacehaven. Was this a similar plea for help? She saw ghosts. If a ghost had sent this boy – God, she didn't even know his name yet – did that mean ghosts in some way saw her, too?

She shoved a T-shirt, top and jeans into the backpack so she could change into dry clothes if need be and wondered how she would get back. It was getting late. It always seemed darker outside than it actually was when you were indoors but still, there was no way they'd make it to the boy's house before dark. And she wouldn't want to walk back alone in the night in a storm. On the spur of the moment – just in case – she shoved a toothbrush and underwear in the pack.

It made her feel sick.

She considered again calling the police, or maybe children's services. It felt not exactly wrong but vaguely *incorrect* to be going alone with a child back to his house. What if there was something abusive going on in the boy's home? Perhaps this ghost and his talk of the Devil were a coping mechanism for a more mundane, human cruelty?

But in the end, she decided not to. There was a whole psychic boulder inside, weighing against her decision. But the boy was here, wasn't he? Someone must have sent him. Someone – or something – that knew she was able to see and, to an extent, understand ghosts.

Someone or something that had been able to communicate with the boy.

She hated it, hated it all.

But had no choice.

8.

He was waiting patiently for her in the kitchen, knees jigging as he tried to sit still on the wooden chair. His top lip was smudged brown from the finished chocolate. He was holding his pack in his lap, gazing at the sheep.

'I'm ready,' said Alice.

He stood up and began to put his soaking windcheater back on.

'I didn't ask you your name?' said Alice.

'Ben,' said the boy.

'I'm Alice.'

For the first time, his lips lifted in a half smile.

'Come on,' she said. 'Let's get you back to your grandad, shall we?'

The smile fell.

'It'll be alright,' she said. 'Don't worry. I'll help you.'

She opened the door for him and he stepped out into the pounding rain. With a last glance at her clean, warm, safe kitchen, she shut and double locked the door.

'Let's go,' she said.

She felt sick.

The Rectory

9.

The rain had let up a little, but the sky was a filthy clutch of cloud, suppressing what little remained of the daylight. The wind gusted over the grey heath.

Alice reckoned it would take them the best part of an hour to get round the other side of the hill to the village of Tiss. The route wasn't easy and they would definitely be finishing in the dark. At least at the last moment she'd remembered to bring her torch and a head lamp for Ben.

For a while they walked in silence, Alice battling the strain of her anxiety. What was she going to find at the boy's home? Could she cope with all this again – whatever *this* was?

Then, as they came between the large grey stones the wind died down and she decided to speak to keep her nagging thoughts at bay:

'Tell me what's going on at home, Ben. What does your grandad do?'

'He was the vicar at our church, St Barnabas, but he's retired.'

'But you still live in the Rectory?'

'Yes. The church was going to sell it when he retired and they offered him the chance to buy it, so he did.'

'And – your folks – how long…'

'How long have they been dead? A long time. I don't remember them. They were killed in a freak event when I was three.'

'I'm sorry,' she said. 'What kind of event?'

'An explosion. They were in a restaurant and the boiler blew up.'

'Oh no…'

'It's OK. Don't feel bad. I don't remember them, so I'm not sad.'

Alice nodded. 'And your grandad has been looking after you since then?'

'Yes.'

'And you say he's ill?'

'Yes. His breath is being stolen.'

'What do you mean?'

'The Devil is stealing his breath. That's why the Grackle sent me to get you. She says I'm in danger from the Devil too now, and I need to get you. Before the Devil wins.'

She was finding this hard, all this talk of the Devil.

'The Devil's not real, Ben.'

There was another blast of wind and rain. Alice watched the boy's face in the fading light. He was frowning, biting his lower lip, stoically facing the foul onslaught of the weather.

'And who is the Grackle again?' she asked.

'Like I said, she's a crazy lady with a hideous face and she comes in my room late at night when I'm trying to sleep,' he said, impatiently. 'Always when I'm trying to sleep. She's scares me.'

Something stirred in Alice, a memory submerged. An image in the darkness, a flash of something grotesque, something turned away from. It passed, like a bat in the woods.

'And she told you to come and see me?' she said.

Ben nodded.

'So she speaks?'

He shook his head. 'No – she kind of…'

They both looked up and off to their left at the sound of a sharp cracking noise. On the side of the dark hill, they spotted a group of people standing around in the heather. Alice could see one of them kneeling, with his – no, her – arms outstretched like some kind of supplicant. Beside her, a burly man in a thick sweater was lifting something high above his head, she could see it silhouetted against a surprisingly bright patch of bracken, a pole, no, a sledgehammer.

She shuddered as she thought he was about to strike the skull of the kneeling woman, but then the hammer came down and hit whatever she was holding to make the cracking sound again.

'Who are they?' said Alice.

'I don't know,' said the boy.

Alice could see others in the group holding poles, hammers, stakes. Were they building something?

'They must be soaked through,' she said.

'They weren't there earlier.'

'Perhaps they're building a path or something,' said Alice. She had worked with volunteers doing similar things at Farthingbridge. But never in weather like this, nor this late in the day. Basic safety regs would forbid it – let alone the sheer impracticality of bringing volunteers or workers out in such abysmal conditions.

'Maybe they're from the farm,' said the boy.

'Farm?'

'Over there.' He pointed down the valley to their left. Alice saw the stone building, the barn with the two large doorways. There was a rough track leading down to it, which they would reach shortly.

'It's unlikely,' said Alice. 'They look like a group of nature conservationists or something. That's just – a normal farm.'

'I don't like it,' he said.

'The farm? Why not?'

He shrugged. 'Just don't.'

They continued on beneath the group, who were so far up the windswept hill they seemed not to notice them. They reached the wider track the boy had been following earlier, the one that came up from the farm then headed around the hillside.

'They're probably building a path or something,' said Alice. 'Putting in steps, pitching stones…'

The boy remained silent.

'But why they're out this late and in this weather, God only knows,' she muttered.

Ben didn't say anything, so they walked on in silence, pulling tight their hoods as the rain squalled.

Alice noticed a young rowan tree twisting its chaotic crown in the wind. For a moment, it seemed to flash with light, marked with clear dark lines.

No – no it hadn't, it was more lightning, surely, down in the valley.

10.

The light was going fast now.

Alice was increasingly irritated by the relentless downpour, as well as… well, the whole damned situation. She should be sitting at home by the fire, enjoying a glass of wine after a hard week's work. Instead, here she was, trudging along, the ground eye-fuzzing, grimy grey, liable to make you stumble, the sky vaguely luminescent, granite grey above the drenched hillside. The boy with the outrageous story following closely in her footsteps.

'How much further?' she asked.

'Not far. I don't know. Ten, fifteen minutes?'

Shortly, they entered a patch of trees and the darkness increased. Alice knew the batteries in her torch were old but she thought she could switch it on now. It would probably have enough charge to see them to the house and for her to get back home as soon as she'd delivered him safely to his grandad. She didn't intend to hang around.

But as soon as she flicked on the light and lifted the beam she froze. The boy bumped into her back.

'Sorry,' she said. 'What's that?'

The trees ended abruptly and in front of them was a massive slab of stone rising high above their heads. Lifting the beam, Alice could see the eerie shapes of more trees leaning out above them. She panned the light around and saw the enormous rock was only one amongst many, all piled up on a small hummock that protruded from the moor, creating an intricate mass of dark, riven ledges and dangling, tangled vegetation.

'Jackson's Rocks,' said the boy, nonchalantly.

'They're enormous,' said Alice. The torchlit grass looked like a shagpile carpet, a giant's fur coat.

'Hm.'

'How could I have missed this?' she muttered, wondering how in the last three months she'd never even heard of this landmark. She liked exploring and these rocks were almost on her doorstep. Then again, often on holidays you fell into a habit of using only one or two key routes in or out of a place. The road to Victor's cottage led down the other side of the moors and every time she'd walked from the door she'd headed east towards a fantastic ridge and never this way, which was roughly south-west. It had always seemed flat and uninspiring to her. Now she knew differently.

'They're amazing.' She said, turning to the boy.

He shrugged. 'Just some rocks.'

Alice swung the beam around. Even in the poor light, she could see the layering of the gargantuan boulders, the way they seemed to rise in several tiers to a good hundred or so feet above the moor. Trees and bushes, black and mostly bare of leaves, soaked silently on its ledges. She thought about the Romantic poets, their feel for greatness, mysteriousness, in the landscape, something vast, beyond themselves. Something which might be there, or might just be inside themselves, their wild imaginations imprinting things on the mountains and lakes before them. There was something of that expansiveness about this place.

'Incredible,' she said.

Suddenly, her light flashed on something above her, through the rain. Movement in the scrub, perhaps a third of the way up, on a ledge overlooking them. It was something large, certainly bigger than a badger or fox.

'Did you see that?' she said.

Ben looked up into the falling rain, highlighted by Alice's torch.

'No,' he said. 'What was it?'

'Something moved up there. Maybe a deer.'

The boy stared for a moment then said: 'I don't like this place.'

'Along with the farm?' said Alice. Seeing the pinch of his grimace, she regretted the tease.

'Come on, we need to get back,' Ben said.

Alice nodded, but instead of walking shone her beam back up towards the ledge. There was something about the way the thing had moved, it didn't feel quite right. It was edgy, swift, like an animal – but there was something different about it. A certain lack of wild grace. It was something a little more awkward, a little more… *human*.

Ben was already a few yards off, beginning to circumnavigate the path around the rocks.

'Hello!' Alice shouted, up towards the ledge.

Ben stopped, shoulders hunched, looking forward. He didn't turn.

Alice shouted: 'Is there anyone up there?'

When there was no response, just the rain lashing her upturned cheeks, she looked down and trudged after the boy.

11.

'That's it,' said the boy. 'Our house.'

Not *our home*, Alice thought, looking down the hillside towards a large, detached house, mostly blacked out by the night except for the lights in three windows – two on the ground floor, one upstairs. From the elongated windows, the suggestion of a gabled roof, the fact it was a Rectory, Alice guessed it was Victorian.

'Where's the church?' she asked. 'And the village?'

'St Barnabas is a little way down the valley – there, you can make it out.'

Alice looked hard but couldn't. Oh, to have the eyes of a child again.

'And the village is a few minutes' walk over that way,' Ben continued. 'You couldn't see it even if it was light, it's beyond that ridge.'

It was now so dark, so miserable, cold, and wet, that Alice could no longer make out the land from the sky, let alone the ridge the boy was pointing to. She nodded and took a deep breath.

'Come on,' she said. 'Let's go and see your grandad.'

12.

They made their way diagonally down through the uneven spring of the grass and sedge, Alice's ankles turning awkwardly on occasion. She was thankful she hadn't twisted one of them on the journey. It was going to be worse on the way back.

They came to a high brick wall and followed it to a wooden gate, which the boy opened. Alice came through after him into the back garden of the house. Quickly she swung her torch around, taking it in.

There was a hunched tree nearby on her right, a dense knot of black limbs with a few leaves still hanging from it like slugs or grey tongues. Beyond that, Alice's torch flashed on a large glass house, with white iron framework and narrow, arched windows. Trays and pots were piled carelessly around inside, overgrown with plants and weeds. The lawn itself was long and scrappy, clearly unmown for weeks.

They made their way down a flagstone path to the back of the house. Ben forced his fingers into the sopping pocket of his jeans and tugged out a set of keys. He opened the door and, as thunder rumbled in the distance, they both stepped inside the old house.

13.

Alice shut the glass panelled door behind her and looked around at the large kitchen in which they stood.

With its speckled Formica units, hob kettle, and warped pine table it looked like something out of the nineteen-seventies. The air had the whiff of damp plaster and faint grey circles of mould emanated from the corners of the ceiling against the outside wall. A red plastic bowl in the sink was chock-full of yellowed plates and mugs. There was a dish with a spoon on the table, flecked with the remnants of cereal. Beside that was a large orange pumpkin and a serrated knife.

'Getting ready for Halloween?' said Alice, indicating the pumpkin with a nod.

'Yes,' said Ben.

'Can't imagine you get many callers here.' Alice glanced at a large clock above the door that led into the hallway. 6 o'clock, exactly.

'You'd better go and tell your grandad I'm here,' said Alice.

'Come with me.'

'I'd better not. You say he's ill in bed? He won't… It's not right, for a stranger to turn up like that, without warning.'

Ben nodded and took his backpack off.

'Don't look so worried,' she said.

The boy forced a small smile and picked the drenched sheep out of his pack. 'You can dry off now, Sheepy,' he said. He perched the cuddly toy on the iron rim, then turned and headed into the hall.

Alice peeled off her waterproofs and examined her sagging fleece sleeves. She heard the boy thumping up the stairs and knew she could do with getting changed. She glanced at the sheep, his drooping face and tiny, innocent-looking eyes. Especially as those radiators are scarcely giving off any heat, she thought.

She peered into the hallway, noticing the threadbare green runner, the herringbone wooden tiles exposed at its edges. The understairs area near the kitchen was partly built out with two doors, their paint chipped and soured to an ugly, curdled colour. A small table stood in a tiny alcove with an old-fashioned rotary dial telephone and a black-bound address book. Like the kitchen, the hall smelt musty and unwelcoming. There were two more doors leading off from it, as well as the wide front door with its elaborate fanlight in the foyer area.

After removing her waterlogged boots and setting them on a shoe stand by the back door, Alice decided to take off her fleece. She listened carefully for the sound of creaking floorboards or the murmur of voices above her, but there was none. Opening her pack, she pulled out the plastic bag with her dry clothes. With no sound on the stairs, she pulled off her tops and quickly tugged on her dry T-shirt – slightly damp around the collar where some water had got in – and her sand-coloured sweatshirt. Next, she changed her jeans and socks and stuffed the wet items back into the bag. She pulled a chair out from the pine table and sat down.

And waited.

14.

And waited.

She looked up at the clock. 6.13. What was he doing up there? Maybe his grandad was telling him off, telling him he shouldn't have gone out alone on the moors, what was he thinking of, bringing a complete stranger back to their home? That was the most obvious reaction. And yet – Alice suspected not. There was something decidedly odd going on here, that was for sure.

This place…

She tapped her fingers on the table, looked up at the clock again. 6.17. Over quarter-of-an-hour. She concentrated on listening. Was that a knock? Something made a sound but… there was no repetition. What was the boy doing?

There was a print on the wall, no, one of those wrapped canvas paintings, a man's head with eyes closed, his skin fiery orange and beard silver-grey, blue in places. A horizontal pole on his shoulders, part of the cross. Jesus, of course. A good painting, Alice thought. Burning and cold at the same time. Passion, anger – and detachment, transcendence. A battle for forgiveness.

6.22.

That was it. She couldn't take this anymore, she was going to go and find him. She went into the hall in her socks, padded along the worn carpet. A shut door on the left then another, ajar, a room in darkness beyond, the front room. In the foyer there was another room off the opposite wall, its door firmly shut. A pendulum clock on the wall broke the silence with a muted click.

Alice looked up the stairs.

It was a long flight, straight up, no turns. The landing above was lit, but only by a weak light source she couldn't see.

'Ben?' she called, uncertainly.

There was no reply. She stepped up on to the first stair, then looked back at the hall, the various doors, for no reason.

'Hello?'

There was still no response, so she began to climb the stairs, using the wobbly banister. The house smelt of old carpet and wood, and something else, something vaguely unpleasant. A sourness.

Like bad breath.

15.

As soon as she reached the landing, she heard the low murmur of a voice.

It was coming from the far end of the dimly lit corridor. Standing and listening, she felt sure from the higher pitch it was a child's voice, surely Ben's. Even though the tone was relatively hushed. He must still be talking to his grandad.

Alice made her way down the corridor, stepping quietly on the worn runner in her woollen socks. The walls up here were more handsomely decorated than downstairs, with a patterned paper of aspidistras and other house plants. There was still a feeling of neglect though, with bulges in the wallpaper and edges peeling away at the ceiling. Alice passed a closed door on the right then came to an elegant little table stood beneath a large but unprepossessing mirror. There was a chipped china dish on the table, dusty and empty. Alice noticed her hair in the mirror, still lank with rain, hanging round her shoulders.

God, what a state.

She came to another door, half-open, softly illuminated by a lamp. Looking back as she passed, she could see a cluttered table with a tassel-fringed light, a bed with a hefty bedspread and… someone lying in it.

It was an old man, mouth agape, his face pale, eyes closed. Asleep. In the calm of the house, she could hear the sift of air through his nostrils. One arm under the covers, the other stretched down his side.

As soon as she'd registered the man, Alice spun to look back down the landing, her interest in him lost.

This had to be Ben's grandad.

But then… who was the boy talking to?

16.

After another pair of closed doors, the corridor turned right and Alice came to what she guessed was the boy's room. The door was ajar. She stopped, feeling a thud in her chest as she strained to hear what he was saying.

'…do now? She's here, isn't she… I don't know…'

There was no one replying to the boy. Alice swallowed dryness. The landing seemed to darken and tilt a little. She reached out and grasped the doorframe, forcing herself to concentrate.

'…it was your idea, how am I…'

His voice was increasingly high pitched, whiny. But he wasn't speaking in full sentences. Alice closed her eyes and felt a giddy spin in her brain, the throb of blood at the back of her legs. Like she was drunk, or ecstatic – or terrified.

'…because you scare me…you're always…'

Who was he speaking to?

'…leave us alone…no, I don't…'

He was stressed. Alice realised she had to act, to go in, fling open the door. But something was holding her back, something more than fear… A nudge in the mind, some kind of ill-formed memory. A presence inside her, in the deep of night, in the flanks of the mind. A damaged creature…

'…you're both killing him!'

Hearing Ben shout, Alice opened her eyes and pushed herself away from the wall. With a deep breath, she shoved the door open and strode into the room.

The boy was in the corner of the bedroom, near the dark window, his hands up around his ears, his eyes shut tight.

Alone.

'Ben!' she said, running over to him.

He opened his eyes. Alice hesitated then, seeing his panic, knelt and pulled him into a close embrace.

'You're alright,' she said, stroking the back of his shoulders.

She felt him shake with one, two, a succession of sobs.

'You're alright,' she repeated.

Alice watched the rain spatter and lash against the sash window behind the boy. There was a faint grumble of thunder, far off, but she couldn't see any lightning, couldn't see much at all in fact except the faint grey patch of lawn beyond the kitchen window.

After a while, the boy's sobs subsided. His breath remained shaky, shuddery, but she could sense he was no longer crying. She kept him in a hug as she said:

'Who was it, Ben? Who were you talking to?'

He paused, as if building his resolve, then said:

'It was her. That old witch,' he said, with emphasis. 'The Grackle.'

Alice drew back, holding his shoulders. She glanced around, saw posters, a desk and bookshelf, a single bed with a metal lamp on a table beside it, the only light in the room. Nothing else.

Looking into the boy's eyes, she said:

'Is she here now?'

'No. She's gone.' He didn't need to look around.

Alice felt relief. Once upon a time, she had trusted spirits. But now, after Peacehaven, no longer. She knew ghosts could be good, indifferent, or pure… evil. Utterly evil.

'She was scaring you, wasn't she?'

He nodded.

'What was she saying?'

The boy pressed his lips together.

'Come here – sit down,' she said.

She led him to his bed, sat him down and perched beside him. She noticed a Transformers picture on the wall, something cut out of a magazine and stuck up with Blutack. Beside it, a black line drawing of a bird, carefully done.

'Ben… how did the Grackle speak to you?'

Again, the boy looked pained. His cheeks tightened in a grimace. 'She kind of appears and… presses down on me.'

'Oh…'

'Then her voice is inside me, kind of… in my head…'

Two possibilities were occurring to Alice.

'And that voice, it says…?'

He turned and looked her in the eye.

'Hate,' he said. 'It says hate.'

17.

Alice looked down at his bedside table, where the lamp shone on a guidebook for birds.

'What does she hate, Ben?' she asked.

'I don't know,' he said, rubbing his hands together on his lap. 'Sometimes I think she hates everything. Just everything.'

Sensing his desperation, Alice said: 'How about we go downstairs and get you a hot drink?'

He looked up. He had removed his cagoul in the kitchen but otherwise he was still in his wet clothes. 'Let's have hot chocolate again,' he said.

'Good idea. Put a dry top and trousers on, and we'll go make some,' said Alice. She didn't want to leave him, so she walked over and stared out of the window as he changed. Beyond the pale shade of the garden, the moors were invisible in the night. As she stood there, another line of lightning sliced the sky, revealing thick clouds, blooming one across the other like mould.

'One, two, three, four…' the boy said and stopped as the air pressed their ears with thunder. 'Four miles away,' he finished.

'I assume that's your grandad in the room down the landing?' said Alice, still watching the darkness.

'Yes,' said the boy. 'I'm ready.'

They left the room and headed back towards the stairs.

'Does he always sleep this early in the evening?' said Alice.

'Any time really. He doesn't sleep well at night. So he's often asleep during the day.'

'What does the doctor say is wrong with him?'

'I don't know,' said Ben. 'He doesn't tell me. But he does have medicine. Not that it does any good against the Devil.'

They came to the man's bedroom and paused. He was still in the same position. Alice could see a rictus grin on his sleeping face.

'Have you seen this devil, Ben?'

'He's not one of a group,' the boy replied tartly. 'He's *the* Devil.'

Alice nodded. 'Have you seen him?'

'Once.' He turned and began to march towards the stairs.

'When?'

'A few weeks ago!'

His shoulder came up as if to keep her away from him. She quickened her pace to keep up with him.

'OK, let's go have chocolate,' she said. 'But then – if the Grackle sent you to get me – me, specifically – you're going to have to tell me everything you know. Everything that's happened in this house.'

He didn't reply but ceased hunching his shoulders, and Alice sensed assent.

18.

Alice set two steaming mugs of chocolate on the kitchen table and took a seat beside the boy. He hunched over the drink and began to trace the swirl of milky froth with the tip of his finger.

'So which came first, Ben – the Grackle or the Devil?'

Ben snorted. 'Like the chicken or the egg?' he said. Then: 'I've seen the Grackle for years, since I was six or seven. But initially it was only once, maybe twice, a year. Now she comes a lot more often. But Grandad – he saw the Devil before he saw her.' He dipped his finger into the bubbles and licked it.

'And you say she's an old woman with… wild hair and a horrible face?'

'Not so old, perhaps,' he said. 'It's hard to say. But yes, her face is seriously gross.'

'Why?'

He looked pained. 'It's like something out of… *hell*.'

'Hell?'

'Yes. Kind of pulped. Big teeth, bits of skull. Like a demon.'

Alice swallowed. 'What does she wear?'

Ben frowned. 'I'm not sure. Old stuff. Not normal clothes. Like… kind of a sack?'

'A sack?'

'Yes. But I suppose it's probably a dress. I haven't looked properly.'

'And she comes in your room only at night?'

He nodded.

'And she always scares you.'

Nodded again, quickly.

'And then does she… kind of *merge* with you… and you hear what she's thinking?'

'Suppose so, sort of. Whatever, it's disgusting. She's a ghost so she shouldn't smell but… she smells.'

'What of?'

'Rotten stuff. Old vegetables.'

'Vegetables?' Alice suppressed a sudden desire to laugh. Kids and vegetables… She realised from his scowl she hadn't been successful in hiding it and said quickly: 'What kind of things do you hear when she does this merging?'

'She doesn't make sense. She thinks – talks – strangely. With an accent. I don't understand most of what she says. Even ordinary words she says weirdly. But mostly she talks about how she hates people, how she doesn't trust them. How they're cruel and jealous and miserly and evil. How she's going to hurt them. Make them pay.'

'She sounds bitter.'

'She is, she's really bitter. She's full of hate. Full of it.' He slurped his chocolate.

'That must be hard,' she said.

Ben nodded.

'And she told you to come and find me?'

'Yes.' He looked up at her. His hair, still damp, was sticking up at the front from when he'd changed his sweatshirt.

'To save you from the Devil?'

'Yes.'

'When did you find out your grandad was seeing… *him*?'

'One night in summer he was very ill, so I took him some soup in bed. But when I got to his door he was up and standing in front of his fireplace. He had his cross out and was holding it up towards the mantelpiece, saying something about Satan, how he had to go away and take *her* with him.'

'Who do you think he meant?'

The boy shrugged. 'The Grackle?'

'Could you see her or the Devil?'

Ben shook his head. 'No. I couldn't see either of them. I think they'd gone by the time I turned up.'

'What did you do?'

'I shouted.'

'What happened?'

'He stopped and looked round at me. He was scared. Startled. He came over and took the soup and told me to go back to my room.'

'And that was it?'

'Yes.'

'When did you see the Devil yourself?'

'A few nights later. In the middle of the night. He came in my room. I woke up smelling old cigarette butts. It was him, standing over my bed.'

'What did he look like?'

Ben glared at her. 'What does the Devil look like? Long horns, sharp claws, red skin. Long tail. You know – the Devil!' He rolled his eyes.

'It must have been a nightmare.'

'Huh.' He looked away at the window then down at the radiator. He swung his head left and right. Alice saw a look of concern, moving to panic, in his eyes.

'What is it?' she said.

'Sheepy!' he exclaimed.

'What about him?' Alice looked at the bare radiator.

'He's gone!'

Alice looked down at the floor, the scratched and stained blue linoleum. No sign of the sheep.

'Did you take him upstairs with you?'

Ben leapt up and began pacing around the room, looking on and under surfaces. 'No,' he said. 'I put him on the radiator to dry. He was soaking…'

Alice stood and began to help him search. 'He must be in here somewhere,' she said. 'Are you sure you didn't…'

'Who the devil are you?' said a hoarse voice.

19.

Alice froze and looked to see a man in a dressing gown standing in the doorway. The boy's grandad.

'Grandad – this is Alice,' said Ben.

'Hello,' said Alice uncertainly.

The man gazed at her in disbelief. Now he was up and awake, Alice realised he was younger than she'd thought. Still old, in his seventies no doubt – but not venerable. His jaw sagged with deep lines either side of his wide mouth. His eyes were small, dark and accusatory. The hair on his head thinned away from the top but was thick and bushy around his temples. He made Alice think of a poet for some reason. Or perhaps a misanthropic prophet.

He looked at his grandson. 'You know this woman, Ben?' he said.

'Yes, Grandad,' said the boy.

'How come?' Alice could hear the dry wheeze as he spoke.

'I – I went out to get her, Grandad.'

'What? In that storm?'

'Yes,' said Ben. 'I went to find her. I think she can help us. Help you.'

The man shook his head slowly. He reached out and put a hand on the nearby counter. Alice felt at a loss for words as he once again regarded her with a critical stare.

'You'll have to excuse the boy,' he said. 'He has these strange ideas in his head.'

'No, it's alright,' she said. 'I was happy to come.'

He looked around. 'Whiskey,' he said.

Alice saw the bottle on the counter near the toaster. Tesco's own. Nearly empty. She wondered if it was an instruction and he wanted her to pour it, but then he stepped mechanically across the room, pulled open an overhead cupboard and reached down a tumbler.

'Do you want one?' he said.

'Why not?'

Once he'd poured them both a shot and passed her the glass, he sat down at the pine table. Alice pulled out the chair opposite and sat too.

'Sit down, Ben,' said the man.

Ben was heading out of the kitchen. 'I've lost Sheepy,' he said anxiously. 'He was on the radiator drying, but he's gone. I need to check upstairs…'

'Ben – are you sure?' said Alice, thinking of the Grackle. Even if she was all in his head…

'I'm OK,' he said, and disappeared down the hall.

Alice and the man looked at each other across the table. She could see his chest rise with the effort of breathing, hear the whistle in his nostrils. The pumpkin Ben had been cutting was between them and the old man pushed it aside.

'I hope I've not come across as rude,' he said.

'No more than I would, if I'd come downstairs and found a stranger in my kitchen.'

'I'm Douglas,' he said.

'Pleased to meet you,' said Alice.

'So tell me what he's done, to bring you here to the Rectory?'

'He appeared at my door,' said Alice. 'He'd walked through the storm. I don't know how much you know about him, his secrets, but he told me… well, he told me someone had sent him to me. Someone, but essentially…'

'The ghost?' Douglas looked up at the clock, then took a slug of his drink.

Alice nodded. 'Yes, the ghost. He calls her the Grackle.'

'Oh, the Grackle, yes. I know the Grackle.'

'You do?'

The man swallowed. 'He's a young boy,' he said. 'He has this imagination…'

Alice watched him. His eyes were dark brown, staring off over her shoulder as he spoke. 'I wouldn't read anything into it. Thank you for coming back with him but you ought to be getting back. It's late.'

'I live on the other side of the hill,' said Alice.

Douglas stared at her incredulously. 'But there's no houses… what, all the way over near Scarman Ridge?'

'Yes.'

'You've walked miles, the pair of you!'

'Yes,' said Alice, 'in the storm.'

'Lord…'

She leaned forward over her tumbler, put her elbows on the table and grasped her hands together. 'Look, Douglas, I don't mind going home. Honestly. It's bloody awful out there, but I'm an intruder – albeit an invited one – in your house, so I'm happy to go. But first I need to talk to you about what your grandson said to me. About the… supernatural things.'

The old man reached up and pinched his brow. 'Go on then,' he said. 'If you must.'

'He said a ghost, a deformed woman, told him to come and get me because you were in trouble from… it feels strange to say it, but… from the Devil. He told me the Devil was taking your breath and hurting you. What do you think of that?'

Douglas looked fiercely at her. 'As I said, he's a child who has always had a feverish imagination. It can make him hard to deal with at times. You really must…'

They were interrupted by the sound of thumping, Ben coming down the stairs at a mighty rate.

'He loves that sheep,' said Douglas, rolling his eyes and turning towards the door.

Alice looked at the radiator. She thought the sheep *had* still been on it when she went up to find Ben earlier. Hadn't it? It was hard to be sure about these things.

'I can't find him!' the boy cried, as he pounded back into the kitchen.

Alice stood up, looked around again. 'You left him down here, didn't you?' she said.

'He's probably fallen behind the bin,' said Douglas, sipping his whiskey.

Alice and Ben looked behind the tall grey bin that stood near the radiator. Sheepy wasn't there.

'Where is he?' pleaded Ben.

Worried he might cry, Alice went over to the back door, with its long glass panels. She looked out at the gloomy garden, heard the rain splashing down from the overflowing gutters. Then she looked at the door handle, realised it was a mortice lock, not latched. The key wasn't in the door.

'Ben – did you lock the door when we came in?' she said.

The boy tapped the outside of his tracksuit pocket.

'Oh – the key's in my other trousers, the ones I took off, but… no, I'm not sure I did,' he said.

Alice rubbed the back of her neck. Surely someone hadn't… no, surely not?

'Is there anyone else besides you two in the house?' she asked, looking down at Ben, then across to Douglas.

'No,' said the old man.

Ben was staring up at her now, his mouth open, eyes wide with apprehension.

'You don't think…' she said.

'Someone's been in!' said the boy.

20.

Alice felt the skin on her scalp crawl. She shivered and looked at Douglas, who was chewing the inside of his cheek. It couldn't be the answer… but what other conclusion was there?

'Is there anyone you know who might have come in?' she said. 'A friend or neighbour?'

'No one has been in,' said Douglas, wiping his mouth as he recovered himself. 'The sheep has been lost, that's all.'

'But Ben left it on the radiator,' said Alice. 'I saw it. I'm sure it was still there when I came up to find him – after he'd gone to get you. I'm sure.'

'Think about it,' said Douglas. 'Supposing someone did come in. A thief, perhaps. A thief foolish enough to head out in the middle of one of the worst rainstorms in years, to come up fifteen minutes' walk from the nearest houses. Do you think he is going to do all that and just steal a toy?'

Alice smarted from the dismissal. She looked at Ben, saw the barely subdued panic on his face. An image of the movement in the trees on Jackson's Rock, the possibly human figure, flashed in her mind.

'Ben, please lock the door,' she said.

The boy went to a drawer, opened it and fished out another key, then locked the door.

'I agree it sounds ridiculous,' she said to Douglas. 'But I think you should just… maybe check the house?'

'Don't be absurd!' he said, twisting a little in his chair with a forced laugh. 'I'm not going to do that. There's no one here besides us.'

There was a pause and Ben said: 'Let us look, Grandad.'

'I'm not in the habit of letting strangers search my home,' said the man.

'Please, Grandad.'

He was quiet for a moment. Then, shaking his head, he said: 'Very well, I'll do it. But the thought of someone coming in out of this rain – it's plain farcical!'

He made to stand up but began to cough violently. Alice hurried to the sink and poured a glass of water. She brought it back and handed it to him as he continued coughing.

'Here,' she said.

He reached out and took it and managed a sip before a further bout of hacking. He sat down and gulped a couple more mouthfuls. The coughing subsided.

'We can do it, Grandad,' said Ben again.

'No,' said Alice, turning the palm of her hand at him. 'If you're happy – ' she glanced at Douglas, 'I think perhaps I should do it. On my own. You stay here and look after your grandad, Ben.'

'No, I want to come with you,' he said.

Alice looked at Douglas.

'You stay here, boy,' he said. 'Let Alice go and have a look.'

21.

Despite her reasoning telling her the Reverend must be right, no one would come to steal a cuddly sheep, Alice decided to do the search quickly as a means of keeping ahead of her increasing uneasiness.

From the kitchen she went straight to the next room, opening the door and flicking on the light. It was a musty study. Against the far wall was a fold-down desk piled with papers, with a few books scattered about on top. The other three walls were filled with floor-to-ceiling bookshelves.

No place to hide here, thought Alice.

She headed into the front room with its slightly open door. When she turned on the lights, she saw it was a large room with two braided sofas, one taupe, the other pale green, and a black-and-white goat's hair rug in front of the fireplace. A few husks of grey wood remained in the grill.

There were places someone could hide in here, she realised, behind the sofas, or at the edge of that sideboard. Possibly behind the long yellow curtains, which were drawn. As she walked around slowly, peering behind the back of the first sofa, creeping towards the second, she wondered whether she should pick up something to protect herself, just in case, something heavy like that decanter on the side table…?

Don't be stupid, she thought. She'd been told – by Michael, she remembered, her almost-boyfriend from Farnborough – that the most likely outcome of arming yourself in a fight is to have that weapon, or an even worse weapon, used against you. After all, anyone who breaks into someone's home is clearly more likely to have the gall to use violence.

She walked past the decanter, held her breath as she peeped over the back of the sofa.

No one there.

Nor, moments later, behind the sideboard. Was she really expecting to find someone?

She went back out into the hall, crossed to the far room and opened the door. Beyond was a dining room with a large oval table and four chairs, upholstered in a tatty pink. She stooped and looked under the table. Nothing.

She came out, headed up the stairs.

She had a greater sense of trepidation as she searched the bedrooms, feeling particularly vulnerable as she got down on her hands and knees to peer under the beds, keeping as far back as she could to avoid being in reach of someone hiding there. She was also thinking about the Grackle. She wondered if she was real, if the boy had actually been talking to a spirit as opposed to a voice in his head. Because that was her second option for this scenario. Ben might be hyper-imaginative, or even suffering from a personality disorder, sensing the dead all about him when in reality they were all in his powerful, lonely imagination. It can't have been easy growing up without your parents, with only a taciturn grandad to talk to. Ripe territory for creating your own imaginary friends

– and monsters. She wondered if he had any school friends.

As she came out of a bathroom with a faded avocado suite, she heard a subdued metallic clang ahead of her, down the landing towards the boy's room. She stopped abruptly, focusing again on her task. Could someone really have come into the house while they were all upstairs? Who would do such a thing? She wished she hadn't seen any of those home invasion films that were all the rage a few years back.

The noise must have been the pipes. An old heating system in an old house. She stepped tentatively down the corridor, switching on the second set of lights, coming to another empty room before turning the corner and reaching Ben's room. She could feel her heart kicking up a gear as she paused outside the half open door, peering through and seeing the bedside lamp, the side of the bed, the posters and drawings on the walls. Hearing… nothing.

She stepped into the room.

Alice glanced around, moved fast past the bed to check the gap between the wardrobe and the wall, dropped to her knees and swung her head left and right, making certain there was no one under the bed.

She puffed. The room was empty. Climbing back to her feet, she looked around at the walls. There was a group of bird sketches, line drawings in brown ink on a good quality paper. She guessed Ben must have done them, he was clearly interested in birds from the handbook beside his bed. She examined them closely, saw how he had carefully labelled them all. Sparrowhawk, Dartford Warbler, Wren, Mangrove Kingfisher…

Common Grackle.

It was a dark, plump bird, gazing upwards with a sequin eye. Was that where he'd come up with his name for the night-time spectre? Might that point towards an imagined being, as opposed to a real ghost?

22.

She was feeling relieved as she made her way back down to the kitchen. She had – with the exception of the attic, which was outside the boy's room and required a pole to reach a hook on the hatch – searched everywhere someone could have hidden. She was confident there was no cuddly toy thief in the house. And increasingly, with the picture of the Grackle, she was wondering whether the whole scenario might be more mundane than paranormal. Although of course that didn't explain how Ben had found her across the moors. Maybe he did have some kind of peculiar ability, some extra-sensory sensitivity, and he knew Alice was the kind of person who might indulge him…

With what? Enlivening a dreary life.

As she veered around the bottom of the stairs, she heard the boy and his grandad talking in low voices in the kitchen. She would go home, she thought, as she walked down the hall towards them. It was what?, probably eight o'clock, and she could be back in an hour with the help of her torch. She hadn't heard any thunder for a while, nor seen any lightning, so there was a chance the storm was abating. And what was the alternative? To see if the old priest would let her sleep under his roof? Ben might want her to, but his grandad had shown no sign of being hospitable. No, she would go home and if there was more to discuss she could always come back in the…

She looked to her left and froze, a few paces from the kitchen door.

The two doors under the stairs – she hadn't checked them!

She glanced back at the kitchen. The boy and the old man were still talking. She realised she had to check these two, to be certain. In fact, now she thought about it, weren't these the most likely places for an intruder to hide, if they'd come in through the back door?

She noticed her throat was dry, and swallowed. Again, she thought irrationally about taking something with her for defence, something heavy. There was a paperweight, a palm-sized lump of onyx on the telephone table, holding down a small tray of note paper. She picked it up and slipped it into her pocket, where at least it was hidden. Then opened the door on the left.

It was a broom cupboard, cluttered with coats, boots, a Hoover, dusty bottles of cleaning fluids. It went back a fair way beneath the stairs, Harry Potter-style. Perfect for the boy wizard to sleep in. And devoid, thankfully, of intruders.

She smiled. Then turned and opened the second door.

A flight of stone steps ran down into blackness.

'Oh cripes,' she muttered. Was she really going to go down there? On her own?

She looked at the wall, saw a large switch set in a metal box. She reached out and snapped it on. A dim light illuminated the space some fifteen or so feet below.

Feeling the paperweight in her pocket, Alice took a deep breath and began to descend into the cellar.

23.

She came down into what she could only describe as an antechamber, a small area with metal standalone shelves crammed with bulbs, batteries, screws, sewing kits, cardboard boxes, old games – all the paraphernalia of a family home. The chamber was lit by a single bare lightbulb sticking out of the wall.

Alice walked to the opening on the side wall, which gave access to the larger cellar. She sniffed, smelling damp brick, rust, old oil. The room wasn't lit, but thankfully there was another switch by the door. She clacked it down and watched as one – no, two – fluorescent lights blinked on in the room.

She was about to step into the main cellar when she froze. Listen first, she thought. Listen carefully.

She could hear nothing. Not just nothing, but a kind of muffling of the inner ear, a severing of hearing. She recognised this, had felt it before, remembering a caving trip in North Thailand where the guide had stopped her small group and told them to be still, hundreds of feet below ground. For a few seconds, maybe a minute, there was no sound. It was like she had cotton wool stuffed in her ears, she began to feel giddy. In the blackness she thought she might even fall over, the silence was so disorientating.

Cellars – and some ancient stone houses like Bramley – were like that of course. But this silence…

She went into the room, to break the sense of unease and hear the faint swish of her jeans as she moved.

It was a broad, rectangular cellar, crammed with old furniture, suitcases, shelves, cans, crates. Plenty of hiding places, unfortunately. Alice began to walk about slowly, feeling the chill in the air, peering around the backs of counters and stacks of magazines and papers, looking under tables and behind chairs. Surely all this stuff couldn't have belonged to the Reverend alone? Seeing a few old vestments and grimy wine bottles, she imagined the Rectory cellar being left between one incumbent and the next, never properly cleared out.

She reached the far wall and saw some hand tools on a table, a chisel, saw, plane, surrounded by a scattering of mostly bent black nails. There were a few wooden crates adjacent to the workbench. Above the bench there was a high rectangular window set in the wall, which must open into an egress well – although it was too dark to see anything through it. The light coming from the nearest fluorescent tube wasn't bad, but still she wished she'd brought her torch to look around the edge of those crates, it was going to be very shadowy there…

She stopped.

The hair on the back of her neck was prickling. A queasiness was growing in the pit of her stomach. The room was silent, she was sure, but somehow in her ears there was a high-pitched tone. Was that an image, flashing on the grey wall? A curved shadow…

Alice lost all interest in the space behind the crates. She spun away from the tool bench and stared back into the main part of the cellar.

And saw him, right there, a few paces behind her.
The Devil.

24.

All she could think was, he was exactly as the boy described.

A tall figure, harsh beneath the fluorescent tube, thick, ridged horns curling up from his temples. A grim, intent malice on his burnt-dark face. Cheeks high and blotchy, eyes small, black and hating. Hating Alice.

His body was bulky, reddish black, his feet set wide apart and yes – yes, there between his legs, she could see it, a long, hefty tail. Hands reaching out towards her, broad and pointed with sharp talons at the end of each finger.

The Devil. It *was* the Devil!

It began to lumber towards her.

Alice's backside bashed hard into the table as she stumbled backwards. She steadied herself with her hand, gripping a metal vice fastened on the edge. She struggled for breath, needing to scream but the Devil… *the Devil was coming towards her!*

Blankness.

Why were her legs folding?

The shock… she was… she was passing out!

Could see him again, moving away from the light, striding towards her, his arms reaching forward and his head tilting gently from side to side, that lumpen face with beady eyes, brimming with atrocity…

God, her head was going, black flashes, she was going to faint. She had to…

Scream.

Alice gulped, trying to get air into her paralysed lungs. She attempted to scream. A pathetic gasp came from her lips.

Everything was mad. She didn't believe in the Devil, knew the Devil didn't exist, but then what was this thing bearing down on her?

As he came into the increasing shadow at the rear of the room, a few feet from her, she felt the power of him, there was a dark authority, he was a serrated twist of feeling as much as an image, with a wicked, overpowering sense of corruption – a tail, he had a tail, and horns, and claws…

She screamed again, louder this time, and collapsed on to the hard floor.

And then he was right above her, still strangely bright and angry red despite the gloom, and in the next moment the Devil lunged on top of her…

25.

There are birds singing in the trees and the Acolyte is there waiting for him at the Entranceway, the opening carved into the rock, reinforced with sandstone plinths. The world is beautiful and he is exuberant.

'This way, my Liege,' says the robed man, nodding his shaven head and beckoning into the dark. 'She awaits.'

'Good,' he says and follows the man through the portal, both crouching and dipping their heads to avoid the overhead plinth which is little more than shoulder height – for a normal sized man.

Inside the entrance the limned ridges and rocky splinters of the cave retreat into the dark. The roof is higher so the Acolyte can stand tall, but he must dip his head to prevent his horns from trapping on the ceiling. They make their way in deeper, into clammy darkness. His left horn catches on an unseen ridge and jars his neck and he curses. Then the light grows again, yellowish, not the silver of the sun, and they come into a large chamber lit by dozens of candles in sticks and dishes placed all around the floor and in niches in the walls.

Two more Acolytes await dressed in white robes. Against the far wall, a woman stands with her arms high above her head. Her wrists and ankles are fastened in chains, which are nailed into the wall. In the centre of the floor is a pentagram marked with the Sigil of Astaroth and he walks across it, up to the woman. She is middle-aged, big boned, with long dark hair. She wears a simple white dress, tied at the waist, and her belly is shaking as she breathes, watching him with defiant eyes.

'Jezebel,' he says and thinking why wait? brings his arm up swiftly and feels a tug as his talons slice her guts like old cloth and stop up against her ribs.

Her eyes stretch and glare into his as her mouth opens and blood bubbles around her teeth.

'You bastard!' she gasps.

She is a long way from dead and he will enjoy this.

Staying

26.

'Alice – this way, Alice…'

God, she was groggy. Some bright light, the smell of damp brick… Her arm being lifted, someone trying to help her up, someone else…

The man and the boy. One on either side. Her head hurt…

'Where am I?'

'In the cellar, Alice,' said the old man. 'You went down in the cellar.'

'Oh…' She remembered. 'The Devil…'

'What about the Devil?'

They were moving her slowly, back through the basement. She could stand, but her legs were weak, wobbling.

'I saw him… here!' She stared wildly around at the cluttered room.

'What?' said Douglas. 'Here? You saw him down here?'

Alice nodded, swallowing. Things were coming back. She wished they weren't.

'Grandad, she's cut her head – there's blood in her hair,' said Ben. He had his arm around Alice's waist, was doing his best to support her as she stepped forward awkwardly. But the old man had summoned a surprising strength and was helping too.

Alice reached to the back of her neck. She could feel a little dampness there. She stared at her hand. Yes, blood. But not much.

'Shall we call an ambulance?' said Ben. 'She might be concussed.'

Alice stopped. She and Douglas exchanged a glance.

'I'm alright,' she said at last. 'I'm alright. I can walk by myself.'

And she could. Without looking back, she walked with them out of the cellar and back up into the house.

27.

'There it is. Only a small one.'

Alice was sitting at the kitchen table, leaning forward as Douglas parted the hair at the back of her head with his thumbs. The voices in the room were strangely muffled, as if she was hearing them underwater.

'Ben – bring me an antiseptic wipe.'

'Where are they?'

'Over there, in the drawer by the sink.'

The boy went and came back. Alice saw a flash of white, a packet pulled apart by old fingers, a glistening patch of fabric pulled out. Then a damp prodding at the back of her head, a slight ache she scarcely noticed. Her head was filling with memories of the cellar, of that creature and the things she saw and felt when he came for her.

'Alice – are you alright, Alice?'

She nodded, without looking up.

'Do you want some tea?'

'What…?' Her voice sounded far away. She heard the rush of water from the tap, the click of the kettle's top being shut.

'There. All clean now,' said Douglas. He folded the wipe and took it to the bin, then washed his hands at the sink.

'Are you sure you don't want an ambulance, Alice?'

'Yes.'

'Or a lie down? You can go on one of the beds upstairs – or one of the settees in the front room? One of us could sit with you…'

When she didn't reply, Ben said: 'Alice?'

'The woman…' she muttered.

'What?' said Douglas.

'Woman…'

'Which woman?'

She shook her head.

The harsh hiss of scalding water filled the room. Alice felt that creature upon her, saw the imploring woman, her pain, the vileness…

'Feel sick,' she said.

'Do you want a bowl? Quick, Ben, get a bowl…'

Within moments there was a Pyrex bowl in front of her on the table. It was somehow reassuring, and the nausea subsided. The presence of the people around her – the old man and boy – grew, as the images in her head slipped away. She sat up and pushed her sweaty fringe from her eyes.

'Douglas,' she said. 'You've got the Devil here. He's in your house.'

The old man stared at her. Still in his faded dressing gown, he looked suddenly drained. He didn't speak, and nor did Ben.

28.

'I need to go home,' she said.

'Now?'

'Yes.'

The rain was still squalling on the windows, the wind heaving against their wooden frames.

'The storm…' said Douglas. 'Maybe we… I… could take you…'

'No. I'll go alone.'

She closed her eyes tight against another bloody image of the woman in the cave. Tried to shut out the sickly feelings inside her.

When she opened them again she was looking at the wretched, white face of a man on the edge of despair, the hurt, confused frown of a desperate child.

'Oh God,' she said.

How could she live with herself if she left them?

'We can't let you go alone,' said Douglas.

She looked at him, his dark eyes, weak, imploring, so different to how he was when she met him.

'You really saw him, didn't you?' said Ben.

She turned her gaze on him. The corner of his eye appeared to be twitching.

'What are you going to do about him?' he asked. 'How are you going to get him out? Because you can, can't you? That's why she told me to come and get you. You know how to do it!'

'Ben…' she began.

'What are you going to do, Alice?' pleaded the boy. 'We need you! We need you to stop the Devil attacking us and hurting Grandad!'

'That's enough, Ben,' said Douglas.

The boy stared at his grandad, a look of incredulity, bewilderment on his face. Alice could see the tears welling in his eyes.

'You need to tell me the full story now,' she said.

Douglas seemed to hold his breath. Then said: 'Yes. But first – Ben, you need to go to bed now.'

'How can I sleep? And Sheepy… I can't sleep without Sheepy.'

Alice winced at the boy's pain. 'Your grandad's right, Ben,' she said, her voice hoarse. She tried to clear her throat. 'It's best you get some sleep. We can look for Sheepy in the morning. I'm sure –' she felt herself shrink inside at the feebleness of what she was about to say, that there was nothing to worry about, '– I'm sure we'll find him. In the cold light of day.' God, she'd never longed for the cold light of day so much…

She could see he was far from convinced. But he seemed to have inherited a streak of stoicism from his grandad.

'I will stay – at least for a while. But we must stay together,' she said. 'He can't go upstairs on his own – not with that… *thing*… in the house.'

Douglas took the last sip of his whiskey. She could see the glass shaking in his hand. 'He – it – has been with us for a while,' he said quietly.

'How often do you see him?'

'Once, sometimes twice, a month.'

'And did you – either of you – have any sensations… hallucinations when he was here?' The chained woman flashed in her mind again and she felt her scalp prickle. Her fingers played with the edge of her bowl. Her sick bowl.

The old man and boy looked at each other, then shook their heads.

'Because I did,' she said. She needed to be sensitive with the boy, to express herself carefully. 'When he bore down on me, I saw and felt… something.'

'What?' said Douglas.

She leant on the table, pushed her cheek into her palm. It was ghastly to conjure the memory, like pressing a fingernail into an open wound.

'He was in a cave. With three men in robes. And there was a woman… she was chained to the wall…'

Douglas drew back on his chair, horror and disgust in his eyes.

'He killed her,' she said quietly. 'It was like a ritual. A sacrifice.'

She looked up and knew her face was taut with emotion - anger and fear and disgust – she couldn't hide.

'Who is he and what does he want?' she said.

29.

Whilst Douglas went to say goodnight to Ben, Alice poured them both a whiskey. She noticed her own hand shaking as she carried them up to the old priest's room, where he'd told her to go. She took a seat in one of the two leather armchairs beside the fireplace, which had been sealed off and replaced with an electric heater.

She let out a deep breath. Her neck and shoulders were tense, her stomach fluttery, unsolid. The memory of that creature, it was… unbearable. But she had to get her head together, to think straight… The appearance, the strange experience she'd had when he was on her – it was similar to what had happened in the past, when she'd glimpsed the memories of ghosts. Like in Bramley and at the Welsh guest house, Peacehaven. Just by moving into the same space as the ghost, she'd somehow felt their most defining experiences, the things that had caused them to stay around in the afterlife. It was as if, instead of her being possessed, she had possessed them. That's how her friend, the Basque paranormal expert, Aitor Elizondo, had described it.

But then – was the Devil a ghost? Or did she have the power to do this with demons too? *Were* there demons?

The prospect was terrifying. Who could say what the afterlife entailed? If ghosts existed, why not more sinister beings?

But the Devil… surely not?

She swallowed and looked around the room, the unmade bed with sheets and blankets instead of a quilt, the selection of pill packets and two glasses of water on the bedside table, one full, the other nearly empty. The rain was spattering against the windows, the curtains still open. She turned back and gazed at the picture of Jesus above the mantelpiece, similar in style to the orange-and-blue one in the kitchen. In this, Christ was standing square on. Alice felt like he was looking at her as she sat in front of him. Looking down on her.

She was agnostic, open to the mysteriousness of things, life's unknowability. She didn't have any firm belief in God and yet she knew ghosts existed, and now she had seen the Devil – hadn't she? What did that mean? Wasn't God the Holy Ghost? Had she been wrong all her life?

The unfathomability of it all swung inside her, an unbalanced pendulum. She was pleased when the retired Reverend appeared at the door.

Douglas came and sat down heavily in the other chair. He picked up his tumbler from the edge of the hearth and took a sip of whiskey, but it made him cough and wheeze. Alice was reminded momentarily of Susannah's husband, Gareth, in Peacehaven, another whose lungs had been struggling, stressed by a haunting.

'Is he OK?' she said, when he had finished coughing.

'Just about,' said Douglas.

'The Devil…' she said.

'Yes.'

They both sat in silence for a moment before she said: 'He's an amazing boy, your grandson.'

'Yes, he is. A good boy,' said Douglas. 'I don't tell him enough. At all, perhaps…'

'Tell me about this place,' said Alice. 'Tell me everything.'

'Alright.' The old priest produced a handkerchief from his robe pocket and dabbed his forehead.

30.

'It's an odd little village, Tiss,' said Douglas, as he slowly buttered his toast. 'A few hundred parishioners, a village store, pub and church. A handful of livestock farms, one a manor.'

'Typically English,' said Alice, putting her hands around her tumbler.

'Yes. On the surface. But there's always been an atmosphere here that's not at first evident to visitors. I came here as the parish priest in the late 1990s. 1997. Moved up from London, where I'd been working in various administrative roles at the Archbishop's Palace for fourteen years. I was fed up with the bureaucracy and politics. I was trained as a priest and wanted a more simple – and visceral – life. The moors drew me, I wanted to walk and think about God and there was no better place.'

'It is beautiful here,' said Alice. She thought of Scarman Ridge, felt the whiskey starting to take the edge off her nerves.

'For a few years everything was normal. I was never particularly good at the pastoral care side of things – I'm too introverted, too interested in metaphysics to deal with some of the more mundane, day-to-day problems of parishioners. But I got along at St Barnabas. It was your usual kind of congregation for a place like this. Mostly elderly, mostly well off, one or two farm labourers and a few remote workers. Only ten to fifteen people each week, maximum. Except for Christmas, of course.

'But then one Sunday a new parishioner turned up. She was a very striking lady, in the early stages of middle age. Her name was Brielle James, as she told me at the end of the service, and she was French. She was renting one of the old townhouses in Tiss and invited me around for tea.

'When I went the following day, I could see immediately she was interested in spiritual things. At first

I thought she was one of those New Agers, her walls and shelves were filled with curios from different religions. Mandala prints, Burmese marionettes hanging from the ceiling, shamanic animal masks, Hindu batik. You get the idea. She gave me tea – green tea, I remember – and told me she had always been fascinated by religious thinking.

'We talked a little about her heritage – her grandfather was Burmese and had come to study structural engineering in Paris, where he'd married and settled. And then we talked about my background. The conversation soon moved on to faith, and my beliefs in particular. I've had a few essays published a long time ago in journals and she surprised me by having read them. She liked my more austere take on things. She didn't say it exactly, but I thought she liked discipline in her religion and philosophy and was opposed to the woolly liberalism that's taking things over.'

'So not one of those New Agers at all,' said Alice.

'No. But as I was explaining my views on doubt and its relationship to faith, she became distracted. I stopped and asked if I were boring her.

'Brielle told me no, it was that she had something she wanted to ask me. Something connected to my faith. I told her to go ahead and, after composing herself, she asked me if I believed in the Devil.

'I asked her why she wanted to know. She became flustered then explained the reason she had come here to Tiss was because of the sightings.'

'Sightings?' said Alice. 'Of what?' She could already guess.

Douglas sat back. He took a sip of his drink, then began to rock in his chair, suppressing a desire to cough.

'More water?' said Alice, beginning to stand.

'No, no,' he said, flapping his hand for her to sit. He composed himself – partially – and began to speak again.

'The Devil has been seen in Tiss for well over a hundred years. Or rather…' he coughed. 'Rather, the Devil has been seen in a few locations in Tiss…'

'This house being one of them?' said Alice.

'Ye…' he spluttered again, nodding furiously. His cheeks flushed.

Alice didn't ask this time, just stood and crossed the room to the bedside table, then returned with the glass of water. She handed it to him and he took a gulp.

'Thank you,' he said. 'And yes. He's been seen in and around the Rectory. And the other place is Jackson's Rocks.'

'Jackson's Rocks…' repeated Alice. 'We came past them on the way. I… I thought I saw something there.'

'Hm?' the old man regarded her keenly, his coughing under control. 'What?'

'There appeared to be someone – or something – moving on one of the ledges. In the shrubs. I thought it was most likely a deer, but it seemed almost… human.'

'Oh, how strange,' said Douglas, appearing not to fully engage with what she'd said. He continued his story: 'Brielle told me she had seen him for herself. She had been visiting the Rocks at certain times of day and night for many weeks. There are local stories, you can find them in books of Derbyshire folk tales, that kind of thing, which talk about the Rocks and the dreadful things that happened there.'

'Like what?'

'There was an infamous occultist here in the late nineteenth-century. A wealthy Reverend who – well, who from the point of view of the Church – went over to the other side. A man named Horace Clay. He was fascinated by the Rocks and their caves, believing them to be a place where druids and other pagans had worshipped. Over a few years he had his men construct various features up there, including fashioning a stone plinth around the entrance to the largest cave – Clay's Cave, as he called it, the name stuck – and creating a natural amphitheatre on the eastern face. He also had his workers carve seats, symbols and other paraphernalia into the rocks.'

The old man sat back and stroked his forehead. Alice noticed how long his fingers were, pale and fine, shaking a little. Nerves, illness, or drink?

'Initially, Clay was regarded as nothing more than a local eccentric,' Douglas resumed. 'Some thought he was doing it all to thrill the tourists coming from Sheffield and Manchester and Birmingham. But then there began a series of distressing incidents associated with the Rocks. Animals were found butchered, their heads and limbs severed, their innards removed. A herdsman swore he had seen a demon appear in one of the cave entrances. For a while, the tourists increased, keen to indulge their thirst for the macabre. But after a year or two the spot lost its drawing power, was replaced by some other fashionable experience. Things went quiet. But the locals in Tiss knew something was still happening to their Reverend.'

He shifted in the armchair. 'Have you heard of the Hellfire club, Alice?' he asked.

'Sounds vaguely familiar,' she said. 'Was it some kind of upper-class debauchery club?'

'Yes. An elite gaggle set up the first one in the eighteenth century, indulging their puerile and immoral fantasies. When Clay set up his own version in Tiss, unusual types began visiting the Rectory. On Sundays, the Reverend's services were noted for their increasingly sardonic delivery and for their focus on Bible passages involving Satan. Members of the congregation were walking out, especially when he began to question where the guilt really lay in Lucifer's fall from Heaven.

'People were seen up on the Rocks at night, lighting fires. Noises were heard, cries, singing and chanting. Then two women disappeared, a farmer's wife and, a few months later, a local widow. A boy fell from one of the upper ledges of the Rocks and broke his neck. He was paralysed and died in bed a few days later from fever. The villagers claimed their Reverend was channelling the Devil himself, and a plea was made to the Bishop to remove him from his post.'

'And did he?' said Alice.

Douglas drew back in his chair. 'He didn't need to. The Reverend Clay went mad and shot himself.'

31.

'Oh my God,' said Alice.

'Ever since, every so often, people see the Devil on the Rocks again. It was because of these sightings that Brielle came.'

'Did you find out why she so was interested in the stories?' said Alice.

'She was an academic, a social historian. Many of our beliefs about the occult originated in nineteenth century France. After years of studying sites at home, her research led her to Tiss, as one of the most prominent occult sites in Britain.'

'So when did she see the Devil?' The memory of that raw, leathery flesh, the horrific face, flashed in her mind. Alice shuddered.

Douglas noticed. 'He is not an easy sight to deal with,' he said. For the first time, Alice sensed the reassurance in his tone. The pastoral side, well hidden beneath the surface.

'She was exploring one of the caves at night with a torch. He appeared behind her, trapping her in. She said she was stunned to see him. To *actually* see him.'

'And the description she gave – it was like ours? The real McCoy, horns and tail and all?'

'Yes.'

'Is she still in the village?'

'No. She left soon after speaking to me. I saw her landlady a few days later and she told me Brielle had gone back to Paris. She'd arranged for her belongings to be shipped back by a Sheffield firm.'

There was a knocking as wind and rain buffeted the sash windows in their frames.

'There's pathetic fallacy for you,' said the old man, with the hint of smile.

'When did you start to see him?' said Alice.

Douglas stared at the electric fire. 'A few months ago. For a while I'd been waking and getting this irrational sense there was someone else in the room. Not necessarily watching me, just… there. It was unnerving, but I suffer from this condition, sleep apnoea, which causes all kinds of nightmares. I put it down to that at first. I didn't make the connection with the Rock sightings until one night last March when I woke and… he was there.'

Douglas shifted around and pointed towards the side of his wardrobe. His eyes blazed, as if seeing him again.

'Was there a light on?' said Alice.

'What? No. It was the middle of the night. There was no light.'

'But you could see him clearly?'

'Yes.' The old priest shook his head with the memory. 'It was as if he were filled with the fire of his own Hell.'

'And he's been back how many times?'

'A few.'

'When did you find out Ben was seeing the other one, the Grackle?'

'I see her too,' said Douglas. 'Frequently. Since around about the same time. She is a despicable creature, her face… I'm certain she's in league with the Devil of Tiss.'

'The Devil of Tiss,' Alice repeated. 'Does the Grackle come in here?'

Douglas nodded, looked down. 'Yes. She is as bad as him. A wretched, wounded, evil spirit.' He looked at Alice aghast, then said:

'Worse even than the Devil.'

32.

The window frames knocked again.

'But Ben said she told him to come and get me, to help you defeat this Devil, who is… damaging your health.'

'Yes,' said Douglas. 'That is intriguing. Why you?'

69

Alice wondered where to start. 'Well – to cut to the quick – there's only a few people who see ghosts. And I'm one. As, evidently, are you and your grandson.'

'I see.'

'But there's more,' said Alice, taking a sip of her whiskey. 'I have a strange… ability.' She saw him staring at her intently, wondered how much of her past she wanted to dredge up. Not a lot, she decided. Not now. 'If I can get inside a ghost, occupy their space, I can catch… *glimpses*.'

'Of what?'

'Usually something that has caused them to remain around in the first place. The major thing. The thing that's stopping them from… crossing over.'

'You could have said that to me a year ago and I would have thought you insane,' said Douglas.

'But not now,' said Alice.

They were both silent for a moment, thinking. Douglas spoke next: 'Does that mean you have helped a spirit to cross over? You can get rid of them?'

Alice pulled a face. 'Kind of,' she said.

'And you think that might be why the Grackle told him to come and get you? Because she sensed you might be able to help him?'

'Possibly.'

Douglas twisted about in his chair, looked at her aghast. Then said in a loud voice: 'Well, I have another idea. I wouldn't trust her in the slightest. I think she might have told him to bring you here for another reason altogether.'

'What's that?'

'To do you harm. Or worse.'

33

In the silence, Alice felt as if reality were changing, becoming more slick, intense. She recognised the precursor to an anxiety attack. Had she been lured into a trap, with the boy the unwitting bait?

'Why do you think these spirits have come here?' she said.

Douglas shrugged. She saw his mouth was sagging. He looked exhausted.

'God,' he said.

She wondered if it was an exclamation, then realised he meant it as an explanation.

'They're here because of your faith?' she said.

'Who knows? It's all I can think of,' he said. 'They look for good to corrupt.'

He looked up at a small carriage clock above the fire. 'Look, Alice, I'm sorry, but I am really feeling it now with my chest. I need to sleep a lot. You're very welcome to stay the night if you would rather that than head home. It's up to you. I know… well, what with everything that's happened, and what I've just said, it must seem like an awful prospect, but…'

Alice thought. She had been through this before, going to bed in a house she knew was beset by spirits. Just never one as terrifying as this.

'Where can I sleep?' Sometimes, she surprised herself.

Douglas sagged down in his chair. She realised he was relieved. 'There's three empty bedrooms up here…'

'I'll take the one closest to Ben's,' she said.

'I believe the beds are stripped,' he said. 'There's bedding in the third door on the right. Would you…'

'Yes, I noticed the linen cupboard when I did the search,' she said, feeling another moment of panic as she remembered the disappearance of the boy's sheep.

'Of course,' he said. 'You don't mind if I leave you to it?'

'No,' she said. 'Is there anything you'd like me to get you?'

He looked at the glass of water he'd set down on the hearth. 'Do you mind refreshing the water?'

'Yes,' she said. 'No problems.'

34.

She felt like she was floating as she descended the steep stairs to the hall. Like she was leaving her solid self behind at the top of the landing. Just taking the ghost of herself – *ha!* – down with her. Everything that was dependable, her resilience, her inner core, was left behind. It would only take a suggestion of that hellish spirit at the corner of her eye to collapse her in a spineless heap.

But there was nothing there. Nothing as she paced the worn runner to the kitchen. Nothing as she passed the firmly shut cellar door. And nothing in the garish yellow light of the high-ceilinged kitchen.

She puffed out breath she hadn't known she was holding and poured water for Douglas and herself. At the sink she glanced out of the window into the garden. The rain was still squalling, spattering and dribbling down the glass. Dark trees and border shrubs ducked and bounced in a wind that sucked and *who-ed* around the old window frames. Branches sprang up and declared their outrage with a shake of leaves.

She was glad she wasn't heading home.

Yeah, so much better to spend a night here with the Devil…

What was she doing? She lifted her arm and leaned against the window, helpless in front of the darkness. She had to do something for this strange pair. Just what? She wished her friend Aitor was here. It was late, nearly eleven, surely she could call him and discuss what had happened? But what could he do now – besides worry? She should leave it until the morning.

Which just meant surviving the night. With her mind intact.

Something flicked, off to the right, near the path. Beside the bird bath. Alarm stunned her. Had it been a foot, the sole of a trainer, someone running away? She stared hard into the furthest reaches of light but whatever it was, it was gone. Surely it was just a shrub moving in the wind? But there weren't any shrubs over there. Her overactive imagination? There was no one there. Quickly, she moved away from the sink, rattled the door handle to make sure it was locked.

Should she go out and look? Shout? No way, she couldn't face it. Her reserves were just too depleted.

She flicked off the lights and hurried back through the hall, shuddering as she passed the cellar door, wondering:

What *had* happened to Sheepy?

35.

Douglas was asleep in bed when she came back upstairs.

He was on his side, his mouth slack and an ease around his brow that hadn't been there when he was awake. She set his water down beside him, switched off his lamp and pulled the curtains, thinking how strange the situation was. Here she was, effectively caring for an old man and a child, neither of whom she had known existed a few hours ago.

A memory flitted through her mind, of her first experience of a ghost, when she was a small child and being read to by a grown-up who simply… wasn't there. She only realised when her dad came into the room and asked what she was doing. Being only three or four, she hadn't been able to explain herself well, bumbling some kind of explanation about the nice man reading her a story, completely baffling her dad. But she remembered that feeling of expansion and security the ghost, or whatever he had been, had given her. He made her feel safe, particularly about the otherworld of spirits and ghosts. Which later she had found – much to her personal cost – to be a mistaken belief. But was the Reading Man really to blame for that?

Ghosts were always there for a reason, some good and some bad. Some were there to protect us and others to do us harm. Just like people. And now she felt that here, like she was here for a reason, the need to protect these two isolated and curiously vulnerable individuals. She felt particularly bad for Ben. At least her first experience with spirits had been good, providing her a little resilience when faced with encounters from the *other side*. His in stark contrast had been awful. How would he cope with it? She feared it might cause him lasting harm.

As she left the old man's room and headed down the dim landing, she forced herself to recollect the trauma of the cellar. She had experienced her fair share of fear, but never known such mind-numbing terror as in that basement. Was there more to the paranormal world than ghosts, the spirits of the dead? Were there devils and demons too? What a godawful thought.

She stopped and pulled open the linen cupboard door. She found a set of cold, slightly musty, sheets and a pillowcase, as well as a rough pink blanket frayed around the edges. Tucking them under her arm, she traipsed towards the bedroom.

She thought about the Devil. His horns, ridged like a ram's. The brutish clump of his head, with the pocked, sagging cheeks. Those eyes, glaring down at her. They were dark, but not black and hellish. Dark like ordinary eyes, small and surprisingly deep set.

She shivered, turned the cold, slightly loose door handle, and entered her room for the night. The bedroom was small, with a single bed against the far wall. Or rather, small in comparison to the other rooms in the house. In most places Alice had lived it would be classed as a good-sized double. She walked across the bare floorboards and took hold of the thin curtains. With the kitchen light off, the garden was now pitch black. But she couldn't help staring, wondering about what she'd seen, the flash of what might have been a foot. About the open back door, and the disappearance of the sheep.

Was someone outside? Were they being watched?

There was too much going on here, too much messing with her mind. She felt overwhelmed and tugged the curtains closed, shutting out the wretched night. She quickly and efficiently made her bed – a skill she'd learnt from a summer job in a Jersey hotel after graduating – then headed to the bathroom to wash. When she returned, she diverted down the corridor to Ben's room, intent on taking a final listen at his door, to check he was asleep.

But the light was on, she could see it at the gap at the bottom of the door.

'Ben – are you OK?' she said quietly.

'Yes,' came the muffled response.

'Can I come in?'

'Sure.'

She opened the door and went in. He was lying in bed, reading his book on birds by the soft light of his lamp.

'Can I get you anything?' she asked. 'A bedtime drink?'

'No thanks.'

'Couldn't you sleep?'

He looked at her, that discomposing look of a child. The self-possession she lacked, which made her realise how vulnerable she was. Surely your confidence was meant to grow as you got older? It felt the other way round. The compromise and dissembling of adulthood took away more than you realised.

'I want Sheepy,' he said. 'I need him to cuddle.'

She realised how important the toy must be for him in this cold, fearful house. She sat down on the edge of his bed.

'I bet you do,' she said. 'We'll do all we can to find him tomorrow. He can't have gone far.'

He regarded her sullenly. She was exhausted, but he must be even more so.

'It's been a crazy evening,' she said. 'But I'm glad you came to get me.'

He nodded.

'I'm glad the… Grackle told you to come and get me.' Again a memory flittered through her mind, more clearly than before, of a sudden jolt in the night, a dark shape, a suggestion of wiry hair. Was it possible she had…?

He glared at her. 'You do believe me, don't you?' he said.

'Yes,' she said. 'Yes, I do. I've seen spirits throughout my life. And I have a special… *thing*… I can do with them. It's like, when I step into them, I feel them for a while. Feel what they were like when they were alive. Do you think you can do that too, Ben?'

He shrugged.

'OK,' she said. 'Sorry. It's late. We all need some sleep. But I wanted you to know I'm only in the next bedroom. If there's anything – anything at all – you need, come and get me. Or just yell.'

He forced a small smile. She felt her heart melt.

36.

In bed. The light out. Her mind racing.

She could scarcely imagine getting any sleep tonight. The rain was thundering on the eaves. She was thinking of everything that had happened in just a few hours. Could Ben do what she could do? Possess ghosts, as Aitor had put it? But there was more. When she was at his door the first time, he had been talking aloud, as if to someone. Could he speak to them too? If so, he was the only person she had ever come across who could. She

77

needed to speak to Aitor again. He was the one paranormal researcher she respected, who she knew she could trust. And he was her friend.

She just had to get a bit of sleep first.

But how could she, far from her warm bed in Victor's cottage, far out in the midst of all this – with the possibility of that despicable *thing* appearing again?

A Caller

37.

She woke in a gloom that was not the complete darkness of night, with a sense of something deeply changed, different.

As her thoughts settled, she realised what it was. There was no more clamouring above her. The storm had ended, the rain had stopped.

She looked sharply sideways, reaching for her phone. The lock screen glowed, showing her the time: 7:15. She had slept!

It had not been a good night, though. The rain had drummed, pounded, softened, then attacked the old house once again. For a while, an hour at least, she had been fully awake listening to it, trying to slow the paranoid thoughts that surged with every squall of rain. Then she must have slipped into a deep sleep, total oblivion, for a couple of hours. She woke, wide awake, at three, convinced she could smell smoke, her heart punching like a fist in her chest. She sat up, flicked on the light, fearful the Devil was back. But no, there was no one in her room, the house was still and quiet but for a light scampering of rain across the tiles above. She got up and went to the loo, then sat in bed for a while, staring ahead and letting herself calm down. If she'd had a book she would have tried to read, but it was too awful a prospect to go downstairs and find one.

After that, she'd spent another hour flipping from one side to the other with the light out, trying again to sleep.

And then, she must have been successful. She had woken once more to the boom of thunder, feeling her gut flare with panic, thinking that damn, that was going to be it, she was still utterly shattered but would be awake for the rest of the night and…

The next thing she knew it was morning.

She had got through one of the worst nights of her life with at least some sleep. She switched on the light and climbed out of the bed.

38.

The house was hushed as she stepped out on the landing.

She glanced down the passage to Ben's room and saw the door was closed. She had left Douglas's door ajar and as she went past could see the room was still in darkness, the thick curtains still drawn. Faintly, she heard the whistle of his breath.

Downstairs, she went to the kitchen and put the kettle on the stove. Then went and looked out of the window at the garden.

She saw the bushes to the right, running along the high brick wall, two crab apples crouched on the lawn, the flagstone path that led to the back gate. She saw the elegant glass house that seemed to have sunk slightly into the ground and… the stone bird bath, brimful and currently being made use of by a flickering robin.

Everything shone with a coating of water in the pale morning light. A few dips in the lawn and patches in the soil beds were filled with puddles. Beneath one of the crab apples a large branch had fallen and was surrounded by a scattering of twigs and orangey leaves. Beyond the garden, the moors, sublime and dust-green, rose towards the horizon.

She found a jar of coffee and heaped two spoons into a mug, poured in the water. Then, her spirits lifted by the daylight, she put on her damp boots, unlocked the door and went outside.

It was chilly but she didn't plan to be out long. She walked down the path, taking care not to slip on slimy leaves, then reached the section adjacent to the bird bath. She tiptoed across, trying to keep her boots from sinking too far into the sopping grass.

She examined the lawn.

There were some shadows in the grass, around the bird bath, trailing towards a large puddle near the back of the house. And some leading away towards the nearby wall and a clump of rangy hydrangeas, each planted in a brick-edged pit. But it was hard to tell whether they were footprints or not. There were plenty of other dents, as well as bits of garden debris all about, the aftermath of the storm's chaos.

She studied the marks again.

They might be footprints. Or might not.

How unsatisfying.

39

Back inside, she stood against the lukewarm radiator and waited for her toast to pop up.

She thought all the radiators could do with a good bleeding, the house was so bloody cold. She'd kept her T-shirt and socks on overnight, but still woke up freezing. It reminded her of Bramley.

The toaster popped up its contents at the same moment as a loud bang came from the hallway.

Alice's heart leapt. Was someone at the door?

As if to answer, the pounding came again. The whole door knocked against its frame.

There was no way Douglas or Ben would be able to answer that. Realising she had to go, she put her coffee down and went out into the hallway.

She could only see part of the wide front door as she walked down the hall, as the righthand side was obscured by the stairs. Even so, she could make out a shadowy figure in one of the stained-glass windows. The shadow moved quickly from side to side, as if warming up for exercise.

Who was it? It wasn't even eight yet. Then she thought: parcel delivery. Of course, living so far from town they'd need to get lots of things delivered. But then again, she hadn't even seen a computer in the study. Nor a mobile lying around anywhere, for that matter. Did they even have wifi?

She reached the door, saw the shadow come closer to the glass, expectantly. Whoever it was would see her moving inside now. She glanced down, saw the chain was hanging unfastened at the side of the door. Should she quickly clip it into place? No, they would hear it for sure. It would be embarrassing. But then again, she was in a house being terrorised by the Devil himself. She chuckled. Hysteria…

She reached out with both hands and turned the latch and door handle. She drew back the door.

'Alright, there?'

The man outside was quite short and leaning towards her. He had a long face, with pale skin and eyes, and his jaw lifted towards her as he spoke. At first she thought he was bald but then noticed his close-cropped sheen of blond hair.

'Yes?' she said.

'I don't suppose you can help me?' he asked. *Supp-onwz*. He had a strong accent, but not Birmingham. North Midlands? Or perhaps the Black Country – Wolverhampton or Dudley.

'What do you want?' she asked. Momentarily embarrassed by the sharpness of her tone, she looked at his hands, feet, glanced behind him. No parcel, box, van, car – or even bike. But he did have a large backpack strapped tight against his black borg collar jacket.

His jaw rose again as he smiled, his teeth surprisingly chunky and off-ivory, tapering at the top.

'I'm looking for…' he reached into his coat pocket, brought out his phone, pressed it alight. 'Bracken Hill Farm. Do you know it?'

Alice stared into his blue eyes. 'No.'

He smiled again. 'I've had a nightmare of a journey,' he said, his accent flaring. *Niyatmare*. 'Been on an overnight coach and then a bus to Wensley. Walking from there, seven and a half miles, mostly in the dark, and this pack isn't exactly light!'

She wondered if he was expecting her to invite him in.

'It's a residential conservation centre,' he said. 'You know, coppicing, step building, hedgelaying – that sort of thing.'

'Oh.'

'Invasive shrub clearance,' he continued. 'Rhodie. Himalayan balsam. That kind of thing.'

She realised she needed to pull herself together. 'I haven't heard of it,' she said. 'Sorry.'

'I love nature,' he said. 'Nothing like the natural world to pull a suffering soul back together. Pure, isn't it? I'm going to be one of their volunteers. Been trying to find a job for ages, ever since I came off furlough, but you know… they don't want the old skills but can't afford – or be bothered – to train you in the new ones. So my work advisor told me to do some volunteering.'

He laughed then his face froze in a grin.

'What do you do, then, love?' he asked. 'You look like one of the lucky ones who's survived all this economic downturn.' *Downunturn*.

'Er, look, Mister…?'

'Jones,' he said. 'Archibald Jones. Call me Archie.' He held out a hand for her and she shook it quickly, noticing an unpleasant clamminess. 'And you are…?'

'Alice,' she said.

'In Wonderland,' he said with a smile and she thought of the Cheshire Cat. 'You know, most people were scared of the Queen of Hearts but do you know who scared me most as a kid?'

She needed to stop this. 'Look, Mr…'

'Tweedledum and Tweedledee. In *Through the Looking Glass*, of course. "But he ate as many as he could get."

They were creepy. And particularly in that 1933 film, the Paramount one that mixed both the books together – their faces! All fat and breaking apart at the jowls like bad plastic surgery. They were bloody terrifying in that!'

'Is it marked on your phone?' said Alice, craning her neck to peer at his screen. 'I might be able to help if I can see it.'

His attention switched as he unlocked his phone, then zoomed the map scale with a reverse pinch. 'Here,' he said.

'Can I?'

He looked up. 'Sure.' He handed her the phone.

After a moment she said: 'Yes, I know where it is.'

'Fantastic.'

'OK, the easiest thing for you to do is to skirt around the back of the Rectory, round this wall here, then you'll see a narrow sand path about fifty yards up. Just follow it that way,' she said, gesturing, 'and you'll soon come to a large crop of rocks. Massive. Head round those and carry on for a mile or so on a track, then it's a few hundred yards down to the left, in the valley. You can't miss it. It's the only farm up here.'

'Thank you,' he said. As she passed him back the phone he grasped her fingers lightly and she looked at him in shock. He continued to hold on for a few moments, meeting her eyes and smiling.

She pulled her hand free and he said: 'Thank you so much. You've been really helpful. And those rocks sound interesting, look forward to seeing them. What are they called?'

'Jackson's Rocks.'

'Like the singer!' He laughed. 'Although we probably don't ought to mention him now, do we? Not after all that controversy with the boys…' He looked at her uncertainly.

She frowned. 'I… I don't know,' she said. Was he on something?

'Well, I'll be on me way, then,' he said and sniffed. He was still looking at her as if he was hoping she would… what? Invite him in? Give him coffee? Breakfast? No way.

He began to turn then stopped and said with a cheeky grin: 'You still didn't tell me what you do?'

'I work in heritage,' she said.

'What, the National Trust?'

'No, Trust for England.'

'You must do quite a bit of conservation there as well,' he said. 'Besides the buildings. They do a lot of nature conservation, don't they? Is that something you do?'

'Not really,' she said, fibbing to try and shut him up.

'I love being outside, the freedom, it's terrible what they…'

'Yes, sorry, I've got lots of things to do,' she said, pushing the door to. 'Good luck finding the farm.'

Again, he looked taken back. 'Sorry, I know I go on a bit,' he said. 'I've got one of those conditions. Never diagnosed as a child but, you know, that's why I never did well at…'

She was peering at him through the crack now.

'Sorry,' he said, laughing. 'He's off again, isn't he? Don't even know he's doing it.' He sniffed again. 'I'll be off then. Thanks very much for your help. I might see you around.'

Alice forced a smile as she pushed the door shut.

She went straight to the kitchen and stood at the window, waiting for him to appear.

After a moment his hunched form came into sight above the garden wall, trudging doggedly up the hill as she'd directed him. She was expecting him to look back but he didn't, which helped settle her nerves. As she watched him turn on to the path towards the rocks, she even felt a moment of guilt. He looked forlorn under the weight of his pack. And he'd had some journey getting here. Perhaps she should have invited him in for a cuppa?

But no, not only was this not her house, she needed to trust her instincts. There was something unsettling about him, which she hoped wasn't just his unspecified *condition*. If so, she castigated herself – then gave herself a pass, because of all she was having to deal with.

And besides, she thought, he was going to that farm Ben had told her pointedly he didn't like. She remembered the group on the moor, doing construction work. Perhaps it was a board walk and they were the conservation group Archibald Jones was going to meet? That seemed possible.

But it was strange. Definitely strange.

'Have you found him yet?'

Alice looked up from the back of the braided settee, where she was down on her hands and knees. Ben was standing in the doorway of the lounge.

'No,' she said. 'But I'm going to keep looking.' The one place she didn't want to go back to was the cellar.

In his starship pajamas and blue dressing gown, he headed off towards the kitchen. Alice jumped up and hurried after him.

'Did you sleep OK? Any more visits?' she said.

'No. Surprisingly, I got a good night's sleep.' He opened a low cupboard door and brought out some cornflakes.

'Is your grandad awake?'

'No, he won't be up until late. He always lies in. Who was at the door?'

'A man. He was looking for Bracken Hill Farm.'

'Where?'

'It's that farm we passed yesterday, the one you said you didn't like.'

'Huh.' He slopped milk on his cereal and then spooned sugar over it.

'Apparently they do nature conservation there, I was right.'

'Looking after bird habitats? And butterflies?'

'Yes, I guess so.'

'Oh.' The boy seemed more impressed. 'That's what I'd like to do when I'm grown up,' he said, cramming an impressively heaped spoonful of cornflakes into his mouth. 'I like birds.'

'Yes, I saw your books. And drawings. I was very impressed. We do some nature conservation in my line of work.'

'Who do you work for?'

'Trust for England. We look after old buildings. But most of them come with big parks and woods and lakes, so we look after those too.'

'For birds?'

'Especially for birds.'

'What's the rarest thing you've seen? I saw a Marsh Harrier at the reservoir. And me and Grandad saw a pair of Black-tailed Godwits last season.'

'I'm not so good on my identification,' Alice admitted. 'Just appreciate the common ones. But I remember someone pointing out a Hawfinch in one of our woods to me once. Beautiful bird.' A memory flashed in her mind, of a black-and-white Flycatcher in the woods behind Peacehaven.

'Yes, I've seen one of them but they're not so common round here,' said Ben.

'Are you going to school today?'

'No. It's half-term.'

'Of course it is.' Before the Farthingbridge fire, she had always been on the ball with school holidays. They arranged their educational activities around them. Now, working remotely on fundraising and comms work whilst the building was restored, she had completely lost touch.

'Do you go to school in the village?'

'Yes.'

Alice sat down with him as he continued to shovel down his breakfast.

'Ben, I've been thinking but I'm not sure what I can do to help. Did the Grackle say anything particular that might help us get rid of the Devil?'

He didn't look up from his bowl but said as he continued to chew: 'No. She just said you would help me.'

'Help you – or help your grandad?'

'No – me. She doesn't want to help him. She doesn't like him.' He stopped spooning and looked up at her.

'Was that what you meant when you told me she was speaking hatefully last night?'

Ben nodded.

'She hates your grandad?'

'Yes.'

He looked down and she knew he was hiding the strength of his feelings.

'Why doesn't she like him, Ben?'

'She says…' he slapped his spoon into his bowl and propped his cheek on his hand. 'She says they're all bad.'

'Who?'

'She calls them the men of the cloth.'

'She hates clergymen?'

'Yes.'

'But wants to save you from danger?'

'Yes.'

'Do you think… Ben – is there a possibility she thinks… your grandad might somehow be hurting you? She might be confused – or just wrong.'

He pushed his long fringe up on his forehead. 'She's got some pretty warped thinking but I don't think so. She hates him but I don't think that's what she means. She thinks the Devil is going to hurt me.' His brown eyes glared at her. 'And she's mean. She says he can have

Grandad for all she cares but it's her lovely *kinchin* she wants to keep from harm's way and that's why she sent me to you.'

'Kinchin?' The way he said it, Alice could almost hear the rhythm of her speech. The old-fashioned rhythm, words.

'Yes, it's what she calls me. Her kinchin.'

'I've never heard that word.'

He shrugged. 'She uses it all the time.'

'So you really can communicate with her then?'

He nodded.

Every time she thought she was getting a grip on the spirit world, something would upend her assumptions. What would Aitor make of it?

'That's a very special ability you have then, Ben,' she said. 'And I need you to know I completely trust and believe everything you say. I realise how frightening all this is for you. But I'll do everything I can to sort it out.'

There was a small sound and she realised he was suppressing a sob. She stood up and came round to him. She leaned down and hugged him, pushing her cheek against the crown of his head. He turned in his chair and put his arms around her waist and hugged her back. Tight.

42.

After Ben had finished his breakfast, they continued to search for Sheepy. The only place Alice paused was when she found herself back at the cellar door. She knew the search was almost pointless anyway. Her main theory had been that Ben had taken it when he went upstairs and then left it somewhere. But that was looking increasingly unlikely. Which pointed to someone coming in and taking it. She shuddered again, thinking about the flash of a trainer – or what she'd thought might be a trainer – near the bird bath.

Why would someone do that?

But assuming the sheep was either lost by the boy, or for some obscure reason pilfered by a burglar, then surely neither of those scenarios required her to go down in the cellar again?

She turned away. But then felt a crushing sense of something… disappointment? Disappointment with herself. By turning away from the door, she was giving in to fear. And she didn't do that. Did she? Oh, for crying out loud, she should give herself a break. It had been a terrifying encounter, but she had to confront it. If she didn't, she would not just be doing an unthorough job – she would be losing something of herself.

She noticed how her fingers shook – actually shook – as she turned the handle and opened the door.

She descended once again into the cellar.

43.

As she stepped down on to the brick floor her stomach spasmed and her coffee swilled up at the back of her throat. She coughed, grateful she had not actually vomited, dismayed that she was so scared she was on the verge of it. She stood, clutching one of the bolted metal shelves, staring at an old *Kojak* boardgame stacked at eye level.

What if he – it – was here again?

There was a little light in the cellar now from the window above the workbench, but she needed more. She flipped the switch and waited for the two fluorescent tubes to blink into life. Then leaned around the doorway and scanned the room.

She saw the chairs and stools, the wine bottles, old vestments, crates, a framed drawing of New York city propped against a Raleigh bike with no tyres. Smelt the musty iron smell. Felt once again that curious, ear-numbing silence. Saw the table, under the furthest light, beside which that creature had appeared. The Devil with the deep-set eyes, the gross, welted cheeks.

Her heart missed a beat, scrambled to catch up. And another. She drew in a sharp breath, never able to get used to palpitations. Young people had heart attacks, too.

Alice weaved her way in between an old Yamaha synthesizer, a tall lamp with a wooden stand, a folded set of curtains, a box full of *Church Times* and *The Garden* magazines. She glanced about, closing her arms around herself against the chilly basement air. She wished she'd told Ben to wait for her at the top of the stairs. Would he hear her if she shouted now? Douglas certainly wouldn't…

She reached the spot where it had appeared. There was the table, an old card table with a green baize top and wooden borders. There were coloured counters scattered across it, Tiddlywinks, as well as a cable reel, the lead unwound and plug hanging over the edge. Like it had been trying to make a getaway, Alice thought.

She crouched and peered under the table. Clear. There was nothing…

She noticed something in the gloom, what appeared to be a light smudge on the floor but could be… something else. She got out her phone and turned on the torch, then shone it on the floor under the table.

There were marks on the floor. Chalk marks, in pale blue. A shape a little larger than the table, but now broken up, as if it had been rubbed out hastily, with many flecks left in the cracks and pores of the brick floor. As Alice traced the marks with her torch, she realised it was a large circle, filled with letters around the edges and lines in the centre. The motif was not obvious but as she stared, she eventually pictured an ordered, five-sided star, neatly fitted within the inner band of the circle. It was sliced through with lines that ended in curves and possibly, on one edge, a cross. Or inverted cross. Looking at the letters around the edges, she thought she could see a T, an O and an A. Most of them were erased.

'Good God,' Alice muttered to herself. 'Who did this…?'

44.

When she came back up, she found Ben waiting for her at the top of the steps.

'What did you find?' he asked.

Clearly her expression was giving it away. 'Nothing,' she said. Then, realising she shouldn't talk down to him, he'd already handled so much, said: 'No, not nothing. There's some kind of pentagram down there.'

'Like witchcraft?'

'I guess so.'

'Was it where you saw him last night – the Devil?'

She nodded.

'God!' He lifted his arms and slapped them against his sides. 'What is going on?' he cried, then turned and stormed off into the kitchen.

Alice hurried after him, clutched his shoulder as he stopped and stared out the window into the garden.

'Has anyone else been here?' she said. 'Visitors? A cleaner? Relatives? Anyone?'

'No!'

Alice followed the direction of his gaze, first into the grey garden, then down to the bronze key in the door's mortice lock.

'The door,' she said, 'is it always locked?'

'Of course!'

'But it wasn't last night…'

'That was just once!' said the boy, shaking her hand off his shoulder. 'There was lots on my mind!'

'It wasn't the only time, Ben.'

They both turned to see Douglas in the doorway. He looked even more haggard than the previous night, but he had managed to get dressed in black trousers and a dark grey sweater.

'That's not fair,' said Ben. 'I always lock it!'

The look Douglas gave Alice said otherwise. Ben, who saw it too, turned and stormed past them both, then ran off down the hall. Alice went to follow him but the old man raised a hand to stop her.

'Let him go,' he said.

'But…'

'He needs to cool off.'

'I've found something,' said Alice. 'Down in the cellar.'

Douglas raised his eyebrows.

'We were looking for the sheep,' she said. 'I wanted to check everywhere. I found a pentagram drawn in chalk down there, with symbols that had been partly scrubbed away.'

'Where was it?'

'Under one of the tables. It was where I saw that… *thing*… last night.'

'Oh.' He pulled a chair out from under the table and sat down.

Alice fingered her lower lip, thinking. 'Who else has been in the house since you first saw him?' she said.

'No one.'

'No one at all? No delivery man, no school friends, workers?'

Douglas shook his head. 'We don't see anyone.'

Alice could scarcely believe it. 'Where do you get your food from?' she asked.

'Ben gets it from the village store…'

After a moment, seeing the man lost in his thoughts, Alice said: 'There was someone at the door just now.'

'Yes, I heard the knocking,' he said. 'But thought no one had answered.'

'I did,' she said. 'It was a man, a guy from Sandwell, who said he was looking for Bracken Hill Farm.'

'Bracken Hill? That's owned by the water company,' said Douglas.

'He said it was a residential conservation centre, he was heading there to do some volunteering.'

'Yes, it is,' said Douglas. 'It was part of a deal to get the local water contract. They funded a group of nature conservationists to improve things for wildlife on the moor. When I used to go walking, I'd see them about occasionally.'

'There was something strange about him,' said Alice.
'How?'

Alice shrugged. 'I don't know. He was a bit intense. It could be me.'

'Trust your instincts,' said Douglas.

Alice nodded thoughtfully, then said: 'Look, Douglas – I'm going to go and clear up those markings on the floor. Then I have to go home to do a few things. But I'll come back tomorrow, on my scooter. I'll give you my phone number in case you need me, I can always come sooner. Is that OK?'

He nodded. 'Thank you, Alice. You are kind to an old man and his grandson in need.'

She nodded back at him. 'Where's your scrubbing brush?'

Jackson's Rocks

45.

Alice made her way up the hillside to the sheep trail.

Despite a murmur of guilt, it felt good to be out in the open air again, away from the claustrophobic house and its occupants. Her lungs filled with the fresh breeze as she climbed up on to the moor. There were patches of standing water, black and shiny, along the path but she splashed through them regardless. As she walked she glanced back towards the house and noticed the church beyond, a short distance down the valley, part of its grey flank and spire concealed by a cluster of bare trees around the graveyard.

She needed to get her head back together, last night had been way too intense. An image flashed in her mind, of being down on her knees under the table scrubbing the pentagram, littered with its odd lettering and symbols. Who had done it? Who had taken so much care with their occult vision? It couldn't have been there since the previous residents. It had to be linked to the appearance of the Devil. Had someone sneaked into the house to do it? Or could it have been either Douglas or Ben, sleepwalking, forgetful, possibly suffering a schizoid incident?

When she got back to Victor's cottage, she was going to make that call to Aitor Elizondo and discuss everything with him. At least when she'd left the house, Ben had been OK again after his sudden outburst. She had promised him she would be back the next day.

She was striding along the trail with her head down, lost in her thoughts, when the sound of a crow caw made her look up. In front of her, the great limestone slabs of Jackson's Rocks loomed, covered by their tangled mess of trees and shrubs.

More images, of the devilish entity pressing on top of her, of the woman struggling in the cave, came back. Her throat constricted. With cold certainty, she realised the memory – if that's what it was – took place here.

She stopped.

Should she go and look around the rocks? she wondered. But supposing… *supposing what?*

Was there something sinister, warped, about this place? Did the corrupt Reverend who Douglas had told her about succeed in some arcane ritual to summon the Devil himself?

She glanced back into the sweeping valley, the dull gold of its grass bent low by the wind. There was nothing dangerous or frightening here, surely? She diverted upwards slightly, towards a point where one of the great rocks slipped under the moor's turf like an ancient meteorite hurled into the earth.

She came to a sloping ledge that formed a natural pathway up the Rocks and began to ascend.

46

She walked up this first rock for a few minutes before it ended at a lookout point between two trees, a good fifty foot above the moor below.

She admired the view, looking along the horizon to a pair of villages in the far distance, then turned to examine the rock face abutting the path. It rose steeply, but there were several smoothly worn nubs of rock rising diagonally that were clearly used as foot- and hand-holds to get to the next ledge. She climbed up easily and found herself on another level area, effectively an elongated triangle, with more slabs of stone rising to her left. She walked alongside them and soon the path curved around on to the opposite side of the rocks.

Trees snaked from the stone, increasingly obscuring the view of the moors.

It was a fabulous place! As Alice continued along the uneven, makeshift walkway, she thought what a shame it was, that it had been tainted by Douglas's tale and her experience last night. She adored places like this. When she was nearly halfway along the stretched triangle, she found her first cave. She ducked her head into it but it was little more than an entranceway, the roof sloping quickly down to the ground beyond the opening. There was a crisp packet and an empty bottle of water at the back. She bent and tucked them both into the side pocket of her backpack. She carried on a little further and, dodging the bent trunk of a sycamore that had managed to grow from the broken stoneface, found another thin natural stairway that led to a higher plateau, back on the same side as she had started.

Alice picked her way up, taking care not to let her feet get trapped in the smaller crevices. She came up on to the next level, a thinner outcrop that promised even more spectacular views of the valley if she could find a break in the dense canopy of trees. She walked along it and came to her first manmade feature, a seat divided by two armrests carved entirely out of the rock. She perched for a moment, but the sycamores had long since obscured what would once have been a great view.

As she was sitting there, she noticed the handrails had been carved with arcane symbols, stars, ankhs, arrows, and one like a horseshoe, the Greek *omega*. She remembered Douglas had said there was a small amphitheatre up here somewhere. She stood and looked up. The limestone was sheer, covered in a lively tapestry of moss, which made her think it was north-facing. She guessed there could only be one or perhaps two more tiers of rock above her. Looking along the path, she saw it narrowed uncomfortably before reaching another viewpoint across the valley. There was a long drop and she felt nervous to go on, despite knowing there was enough room to walk normally, without having to hug the wall. Still. She wouldn't come off well if she slipped, and the stone was still damp from the storm. And slimy in places, with moss.

But she was keen to find out what was on the other side of the rock, and whether there was a way up to the very top, which couldn't be far off now.

She moved forward quickly, determined not to think about it.

Soon she was on the far side of the narrow section, her heart fluttering. She took a moment, propping herself against the rock with one hand and looking down at the slabs of stone below. With the shrubs, not a nice mix to fall on to, that was for sure.

And then, as if on cue, she felt the presence of something moving behind her, a figure, right behind her, leaving the narrow ledge, plunging quickly.

She gasped and spun, having time to catch the sense of someone – a pale blond youth? – flinging themselves away from the edge, plummeting…

Alice shrieked, reaching for the bright figure –

Only to find herself clutching at nothing, stumbling back on to the narrow lip of rock, panicking, grabbing at the rockface to steady herself but instead slipping, one of her feet coming off the ledge, a sensation of weightlessness and then she knew she was going over, this was it, she was lost, but her hand came out and caught a rocky protrusion, her arm locked round it and–

She stopped falling.

Her legs were completely off the edge but her right arm was tight around the cone of rock like a stalagmite and she was stable, not moving, not plunging to her death on the treacherous mix of branch and stone below.

She felt a surge of debilitating panic, draining her legs and belly of strength. She gripped the rock tighter, right up against her cheek, feeling the roughness of the stone.

OK. She was OK. She needed to get her legs back up and inch back a little and she would be safe. Completely safe.

Carefully, she twisted her hips and raised her left knee, feeling for the edge of the path, looking down at trees but unable to see her leg because she dared not move her face away from the protruding rock. Her arm was locked safely enough around it, but it was only a small outcrop, with no margin for error. If she leaned away the crook of her elbow might slip, especially as the stone was still damp and slick with rain and moss.

Had that been a boy falling?

She would look down as soon as she was safe. It couldn't have been a boy, there was no one else around, but there had been something… A bird? Something larger? A deer? No, a human, she was sure. And yet…

Her knee connected with the path. Clutching the protrusion with her other hand, she pushed herself backwards and was once again on the wider section of path. She scuttled further back on all fours until her back was pressed against the rockface and both her feet were planted firmly on the ledge.

She waited for her breathing to calm and then stood and peered over the ledge. She half expected to see a broken form down there and… half didn't.

There was no one there. Nothing there.

'Hello?' she called.

Nothing. There was no disturbance at all. She had imagined it. She knew she had imagined it.

Or was it a ghost?

She remembered the pale shape she had seen on the Rocks the night before.

She scanned the area below again. There was nowhere a body could be lying hidden in the rocks. She would see him, that was for sure.

So it had to be her imagination, an incorrect functioning of the brain.

Or a ghost.

Despite her anxiety, she took a deep breath and decided to carry on.

47.

She soon found more of the strange symbols, this time carved straight into the side of the rock. Within a series of joined strikes was a picture of a stylised bird in profile, gazing sternly at her. A bird of prey, oddly reminiscent of an American eagle.

As she came through a clutch of oddly angled trees, she found herself at the edge of the amphitheatre Douglas had mentioned.

It had three long, curved seats, running down to the performance area. The workers had done a neat job under the challenging circumstances. There were a few odd lumps and bulges – and the stage was shaped like a comic speech box as opposed to a neat circle – but she could easily imagine a couple of dozen people sitting here at night by candlelight, watching a quirky, two-person performance of The Tempest, or some Joan Baez lookalike performing with a guitarist.

It was cool.

Alice clambered down over the seats and followed the route through a gap between the broken rocks at the far side of the amphitheatre.

48.

She came to the cave.

That cave. The one she had seen in the horrific moment shared with the entity in the cellar. With the Devil.

The rough, natural opening had been set with sandstone blocks on either side, balancing a single plinth across the top. Mortar filled the gaps, fashioning a neat rectangular doorway that Alice would only need to duck her head to pass through.

She remembered the man, bald, in white robes, waiting. She saw his sallow face, a squint, she now recalled, in his left eye, a dark mole high on his temple. Remembered being in *him*, the demon, how he had crouched and dipped his horns – his *horns* – to enter this place.

She felt a turn in the air. A chill with no breeze. Just her, her skin reacting to the memory, hair follicles tensing like filings to an icy magnet. Could she go in?

The sandstone blocks seemed to brighten in front of her, becoming vivid, somehow more real. She could see the tiny grains, the powdery, brownish-yellow surface. She could smell damp stone, the musty cave, something of the leaves and trees, an iron-like quality to the air. This place…

The Devil was gone now. But Douglas had told her about Brielle, the Frenchwoman, how she had seen him up here…

With a deep breath, Alice ducked and entered the cave.

49.

Inside, the rock he had weaved around, jagged and broken like it would claw you.

Her lungs tightened. Air would only reach the very top of her chest.

She moved forward, one, two, three steps – and her neck jarred sharply to the right. She felt a sickly anticipation in her stomach, remembered how his ram's horn had snagged against the roof. Just here. There was a growl, an angered sound memory, deep in her ear. Her hand came up to the back of her head, she rubbed her hair, felt dampness, sweat there. It was cold but she was hot.

Her eyes strained against the fading of the light, the further she moved into that despicable hole in the rock. She stopped and took off her pack, noticing how her fingers shook as she rummaged around in it for her torch. After a moment, she cursed – it wasn't there! She must have left it at the Rectory. She remembered other important times when she'd lost or forgotten things. Her penknife when she needed it for the Caravaggio in the Farthingbridge fire, her door key when she got back from the Lakes to Bramley… she was hopeless!

Thank God she had her phone. She reached into her back pocket, drew it out and flicked on the torch. Then groaned as she noticed the red line telling her the battery was low, just 4%. Not surprising, she had left her charger in the cottage, and the battery was old…

But she should only need it for a short while.

She took another deep breath and shone it around, the harsh beam finding lips of rock, the narrowing gap running further back, something moving, no, just the torch on frozen stone. Alice took more steps onwards, feeling increasingly horrified, not by the thought of the Devil but by the strangeness of what was happening inside her. There was a growing sense of anticipation, something she could barely relate to… a cruelty, a perversely *sexual* desire, creeping up within. She wanted something dark, something sublime to happen, a breaking of life's rules, of day-in, day-out ordinariness, of the humdrum nature of existence. She *wanted* another's fear, hurt…

There was a clattering sound, she propped herself against a wall.

'Shit!'

It was dark. Because she'd dropped her phone and was clutching her forehead with both hands.

She stooped and fumbled in the gloom. Found the phone and flipped it over, brightening the ceiling and walls once again with its fierce little light. She traced the glass with her thumb, praying it wasn't shattered, but it felt smooth, whole, although, with the screen light she could see a thin crack. And the battery level, 3%.

'Shit,' she said again.

Ignoring the ghastly sensation in her stomach, the insidious craving at the back of her mind, she walked on swiftly, swerving away from rough rock, steadying her balance as the floor dipped, coming through into a larger space, the place where the woman had been chained, oh it was clear, this was the place, she remembered the candles, the shaven-headed men in robes, the chains on the walls, the woman's defiant gaze that had so swiftly changed when…

'No!' she shouted, feeling his feelings, sensing his thoughts, clenching her free hand as if it to deny its talons, to prevent it from coming up and slicing the soft stomach…

Clenching her teeth against waves of heat, desire, revulsion, Alice directed the torch beam at the wall, saw shadows flitter like bats, realised she had to move fast, couldn't waste the battery, needed to get out by its light, saw high up, *there*, a smooth, black, solid shape. She advanced and stared at a rusted metal ring driven into the stone, imagined the chain that once hung there.

Her stomach wretched and she gulped back bile in her throat.

She bent over, again clutching the wall to steady herself. An image of the woman's eyes, defiant, scared, then dazzled with the shock of a fresh new pain…

The mad ecstasy of violence. A joyous rupturing of the bonds of sanity.

Alice stumbled left and right, fell to her knees near the ring. Her torch flashed behind an outcrop and she noticed a small, concealed passage, leading off from the cave into deeper darkness.

She cried out, an inchoate noise, and ran from the chamber, clutching her belly.

50.

Outside.

Her back pressing against stone. Her head tilting to suck air back into her lungs. Hands shaking, feeling at her face, dabbing wetness from her cheeks, her eyes.

I am me.

Alice. She was not that thing. That Devil. She was Alice Deaton.

She didn't hate, didn't kill. She loved people, loved women.

The leaves and branches ceased to whip and swirl before her, her darting eyes slowing, steadying.

She focused on one thing, a patch of straw-coloured grass, bright in between the crook of two tree trunks.

Straw. Like a snow globe, her thoughts began to settle. With them, her raw, tortured feelings.

It had been a momentary merging, a memory attached to the place, to her experience in the cellar, made possible by her ability to connect with spirits. Because of that, it would pass. Wouldn't it?

'Why me?' she whispered. Why did she have to have this strange power? And then she heard an incongruous sound, a metallic clank, echo in the air around her.

She wondered if it was real, or something else attached to her unwanted, inexplicable experience. She needed to get down, go back, get home. Needed the clarity and sanity of her own space. Needed to recover.

She turned away from the crafted portal and began to head back down the Rock.

51.

There was another route down on the far side of the amphitheatre, a broader, gentler set of ledges and steps that meant she could avoid the laborious, concentric path she'd followed up.

Concentric like Dante's Hell, she thought, as she headed down. Any romantic notion of Jackson's Rocks had been eliminated by her experience in the cave. She was never coming back here.

The last stretch off the Rock was a mixture of soily patches and littered stones, dense with shrubs and rusty fronds of bracken. It was as she was passing through here she heard again the metallic clanging sound, like swords striking.

She slowed as she noticed another, softer sound – someone talking.

There was a large boulder ahead, blocking her view of the speakers. Who could it be?

As she crept towards the rock the person spoke again, a woman's voice, and someone chuckled in response. Alice felt the tension in her shoulders drain. She straightened her back and walked around the path in between the rock and a patch of grass knotted with bramble.

As she came round the giant boulder she stopped, finding herself facing a group of people standing about in the woody scrub. There was an old man and woman, a tall young man with glasses, a couple of younger women and, a short way off near a tree… the man who'd called at the Rectory door that morning.

Archibald Jones.

'Oh…' she muttered, as they all stopped and stared at her.

She gaped at them, her brain whirling as it took in the bizarre combination of weapons they were wielding – wooden poles with hefty blades on the end, saws, short-handled scythes – then realised who they were.

The conservationists.

'Hello again!' cried the pale blond man, Archie. He lifted his slasher in the air in greeting.

'Uh - hello,' said Alice.

'Fancy seeing you here!' Archie rested the slasher on his shoulder and began to walk towards her.

'Do you know this lady?' said the old woman, oval-faced and with her hair tied in a bun. There was a dark, rusty sickle in her gloved hand. She smiled at Alice.

'Yeah, met her this morning,' said Archie. 'She told me how to get to the farm.' He smiled, showing his large teeth, as he drew up in front of Alice. 'As you can see, I didn't make it,' he said to her. 'Met them on the way. That's synchronicity, or something.'

'Yes, something,' said Alice, quietly.

They stared at each other, then Archie shook his shoulders, grinned again, and gestured towards the group. 'Let me introduce you to the Elder Moor Conservation Volunteers,' he said. 'Alice – how could I forget that one? – this is Jem, short for Jemima,' he tipped his head at the old woman. 'Charles…' The slight, balding old man beside Jem gave Alice an eager nod. 'Blake…' The giant man with thick hair and black rimmed glasses, a pot belly showing under a faded Kings of Leon T-shirt. 'Stella and Leanda,' The younger women, both with a Mediterranean hue to their skin, smiled. 'They're sisters,' he added.

'Cousins,' said the one with her black hair in a ponytail, in what Alice thought was a Greek accent.

'Nice to meet you,' said Alice. She looked around at the rest of the group, to include them all.

'Do you live in Tiss, Alice?' asked the old woman, Jem.

'She lives at the Rectory,' said Archie proudly.

Alice winced. 'No – I don't live there. I was visiting some… one. I'm staying in a cottage over the other side of the moor.'

Archie drew his head back sagely. 'Alice is in our line of business,' he said. 'Works for the National Trust.'

'Trust for England,' said Alice.

'Oh, how lovely,' said Charles. 'Jem and I are both members. What a fabulous place to work, saving our beautiful heritage.'

'Yes, we spend a lot of weekends visiting the local houses,' said Jem. 'Crickhurst is lovely. Although those latest exhibitions, all about the slavery and lesbians…'

Alice didn't need this. 'The history is the history,' she said, glancing around for the best way through the group.

'But there's so much of it, isn't there?' said one of the younger women, Stella or Leanda. 'Which bits the culture chooses to highlight, that's what's interesting, isn't it?'

'Yes, you're absolutely right,' said Alice. She would need to take the main path, right through the middle of them, in between Charles and Blake. Her emotions were still in turmoil from the cave. She began to walk forward, in between them.

'You off home, then?' said Archie as she walked past him.

'Yes,' she said. And then, feeling awkward she was showing so little interest in them, added: 'What are you guys up to here?'

'Clearing back the vegetation, opening up the paths to the Rocks,' said Blake, in a deep Lancashire accent. 'I love nature,' he added, putting a hand on his hip.

Alice suppressed a fleeting desire to snort with laughter. It was the kind of thing surely taken for granted these days. Saying it almost felt like parody. Hadn't Archie said something similar?

'And you're all at Bracken Hill farm?' she said, managing to control herself.

'Not us,' said Charles, as the younger members of the group all nodded. 'We live in Wigtwizzle.'

'We drive out to join them whenever we can,' said Jem.

'The Water Company funds you, doesn't it?' said Alice, directing the question at Blake.

'That's right,' said the big man. 'They give us tools and materials, and a couple of vehicles.'

'They pay some of the running costs, too,' said Charles. 'Heating, water bills…'

'They need to scrap the Land Rover,' said the other of the two Mediterranean women, her voice deeper, huskier than her cousin's. 'Bloody rust bucket!'

Blake laughed.

'Would you like a brew?' said Jem. 'We're about ready for our break.'

'Uh – no thanks,' said Alice. 'I have to get back…'

The woman gave Alice a warm smile as she walked on, in between the old couple. Alice's eye was drawn again to the thin, blackened curve of the sickle that hung loosely in her gloved hand.

'You're always welcome to join us, Alice,' said Archie. 'If you fancy keeping your hand in with the old outdoor work?'

'Thanks,' said Alice. 'I'll let you know.' She waved to him as she headed through into the thin stand of trees beyond the motley group.

As she followed the trail through the trees, she was thinking about how Archie seemed to have fallen naturally into a leadership role in the group when something small and devilishly fast broke from the bracken and darted across the path. Alice shrieked before realising it was nothing more than a squirrel, then felt herself flush with embarrassment. The group certainly would have heard her.

She hurried on, only later wondering as she broke out on to the open moor why none of them had come to check she was OK. There was a vehicle parked on the edge of the wood, one of those old series 2 Defender station wagons with long benches in the back. Alice had spent plenty of time in similar Land Rovers, often packing them with more than the officially sanctioned seven passengers. She'd managed to get twelve volunteers in once, without too much trouble. Not that she'd do that now, of course, with all the training she'd had since.

52.

When she got back to the house she plugged in her phone and made herself a strong coffee. Then she lit the fire in the lounge and sat down on the sofa. She stared out of the small, high window at the grey sky and tried to think of… nothing.

She needed to empty her mind. Clear it of those sick images, the rotten sense-impressions, corrupt feelings. It felt like there was a dirty fight at the back of her head, a competition between foul memories for the window of consciousness.

She wondered if it was too early for wine.

Yes. It was only 2.30.

Her world had been upturned a few times in her life, but this was the strangest of all. The boy sent to her by the Grackle, the old priest haunted by the Devil, the disappearance of the cuddly sheep, the wretched experiences in the cellar and the cave… And that man, Archibald Jones, and the rest of his strange group.

Up until yesterday, working up here had been fun, a bit like a holiday, giving her some much-needed rest and healing time… but not anymore. Now it was a nightmare.

By the time she'd finished her coffee, the phone had gained enough charge for her to call her friend, Aitor.

'Darling!' She felt herself break into a smile, hearing that Iberian enthusiasm.

'Are you still at work?' she asked. It was Friday afternoon, she knew he finished his job at the Research facility early on Fridays.

'Yes. Sounds like you're not just ringing for a chat? Shall I call you back when I finish – in say, half an hour?'

'Yes, that would be good,' she said. 'Please do, Aitor. I need to talk to you.'

'Of course,' he said. 'I'll make it twenty minutes.'

'Great.' She ended the call and stared at her screen. *14:34. Fri, 29 October.*

53.

When Aitor called back she told him the full story, from the appearance of Ben in the storm to the horrific sense-memory of the Devil and the woman in the cave. She also told him about the strange conservationists.

'Alice, you need help with this,' he said when she'd finished.

'Yes I do.'

'My mother is with me this week,' he said.

'Over from San Sebastian?'

'Yes. But… but, but, but… let me see… I will have to tell her to amuse herself for the next couple of days…'

115

'Aitor – you can't do that!'

'She'll be fine. Honestly. I wouldn't say it if I didn't mean it. She has the independent Basque country spirit. She'll be off to London in no time. On her bike.'

'Bike?'

'Motorbike. A Honda 750X, she takes it everywhere.'

Alice laughed. 'But how often do you see her?'

'At least twice a year. She comes here for a fortnight and I go there, usually for a couple of weeks, too.'

'Aitor…'

'Alice, I don't think you've listened to yourself. You've done your possession thing with *the Devil!*'

She didn't say anything.

'I'll drive up first thing tomorrow morning. I'll be up by lunchtime.'

'Thank you. Tell your mum I'll make it up to her.'

'You must come and meet her. In San Sebastian. You would love her. She would love you!'

'I will, promise. Thank you, Aitor…'

54.

How do you rationalise an encounter with the Devil?

Alice didn't believe in God. She had always thought she was too small, too limited, a part of the universe to make big decisions like that. But if the Devil could appear in a cellar in a small Peak District village, then what about Angels too? She knew from her experience ghosts existed, so why not the whole caboodle? God, Satan, cherubim and seraphim, or whatever they were called?

Sitting there on the sofa, staring into the crackling and spitting fire, she felt the fingers of panic in her mind. She mustn't let the floodgates open. Who knew where she would end up, spiritually and emotionally? She remembered the appalling time she'd had as a teenager, on the verge of breakdown after her dad's accidental death and her friend Susannah's betrayal. And this, this experience of – with, *in* – the Devil was worse. Why?

With a shudder, she knew why. The thing that was petrifying about him wasn't that he was an agent of evil, but that he was a catalyst of it. True, he was terrifying. But what was even more terrifying was how he showed her something inside herself, a pit of black, a capacity to feel and imagine evil she'd never known was there.

It was as much *her* she was frightened of as him.

She shut her eyes. One thing at a time.

She needed to get to the bottom of Tiss and Jackson's Rock, there was a mystery here and she would resolve it – with the help of Aitor. That was her hope, that was where she would stake –*retain* – her sanity.

What was the alternative?

She went into the kitchen and tidied up her work, the mess she'd made keeping to her deadline that felt like a lifetime ago, all the mixed-up printouts, empty cups, used tissues, the plate with banana skin and honey splodges. Keeping herself busy to steady her mind, she headed upstairs, sorted all her washing and put it on, then thought about the sleeping arrangements. She wanted to give Aitor the main bedroom but, with only one change of sheets, decided to pull hers off and put them in the second bedroom, then remake the main bed. She could do it tomorrow but felt she may as well get it out the way now, while she needed to occupy her mind. She took her

117

book and hairbrush into the smaller room, which looked out tight against a high retaining garden wall. It was nowhere near as nice as the front bedroom with its views down the valley, and there was no room for anything except the single bed, so she would have to leave her clothes in the wardrobe.

But Aitor was easy going, he wouldn't mind that.

55.

By the time she had finished readying the house, it was properly dark outside.

Staring out of the living room window into the blue-black, Alice realised she had only once or twice pulled the curtains since she'd moved up here. But now she thought of the Devil and Archie Jones and those conservationists and decided she would close them all throughout the house. Turn on the lights in your house at night and it was like being on the big screen for anyone looking in from outside. They could see you clearly whilst you couldn't see them. And say there was someone lurking outside, someone unsavoury, and say they did for some sinister reason break in, her nearest help was about three-quarters of a mile away. And that was… Bracken Hill Farm.

How quickly could the police get here? Were there cars in the villages, Edale or Hope? Or would they have to come from the biggest town, surely not all the way from Glossop – or Sheffield?

'Stop it, Alice, they're conservationists, for God's sake,' she muttered to herself. There was no point in thinking like that. And anyway, she only had one more night alone – for now. Aitor would help her through this strange situation. Wouldn't he?

Rain lashed against the windowpanes. Faintly, she could see the hawthorn by the garden wall wobble about in a new breeze. She hoped the storm wasn't going to come back as she drew the curtains, shut out the night. She thought about Douglas and Ben in that big old house, Douglas most likely in bed, probably asleep, Ben poring over his bird books to keep the Devil and Grackle out of his mind.

She had to help them.

But for now, she needed to fill a few more hours before bed and then, hopefully, get a good night's sleep.

She went around the house shutting all the other curtains, then settled down in the living room with the fire, candles, a glass of wine and a US drama on Netflix.

56.

'Make an incision and squeeze some of that out…'

'Will he need anaesthetic?'

'Just local.'

'My boy…'

Alice opened her eyes, took in the TV glare, burned down candles, husks of wood glowing on the fire. She picked up the remote and paused the show, her eyes flicking to the corner of the screen to see she was not one but two episodes ahead of where she'd started. A little wine must have knocked her out. Her head was bent awkwardly against a cushion where she'd half-lain across the sofa, feet up on a stool. She felt her neck crick painfully as she raised it.

She turned off the TV and sat up, massaging the back of her head and feeling the scab from when she'd fallen in the cellar. She shivered thinking, she was a woman who had seen the Devil. *Been inside the Devil.*

With the TV dead and the fire and candles mostly burned out, the room was gloomy and cool. She hadn't bothered putting the heating on and her body temperature had dropped while she was sleeping. She needed to get to bed, to snuggle down and get some proper sleep.

Alice switched on a side light and then snuffed out the candles with finger and thumb. She picked up the poker and stabbed the orange filigree on the smouldering logs, then set the guard in front of the fire.

Still groggy, she traipsed up the steep narrow staircase, realised she couldn't be bothered to brush her teeth, pushed open the door to the *cupboard* bedroom.

And screamed at the sight of the thing in her room.

57.

It was sitting on her bed, a mass of wiry, seemingly wriggling, dark hair around its face – or rather, what was left of its face. Alice stood, her frame shaking as she hyperventilated, struggling to see, to truly see, the creature before her.

It was a ghost, that much was clear from the vague, phosphorescent light that limned the curve of its shoulders, the spray of its hair, the knees clamped together in a dreary sheet, no, a dress. It was a woman spirit, bedraggled, poor, and with the most atrocious injury. Alice forced her gaze on to that ragged, torn face, the cheeks patched with a smooth whiteness – bone! – the black mouth with long, gum-less teeth. The dabs like plasticine all around that were… what remained of her flesh.

The woman's face had lost most of its skin. Had it rotted away? Alice's hand came up to her mouth as she stood in front of the bent-over creature, her eyes repeatedly flicking away to the dark walls as she tried to cope with the sight of her.

'What happened to you…?' she whispered, thinking, was it leprosy?

Slowly, the woman's head lifted and her eyes, white amidst the jellyish crimson and orange of her brow and cheeks, fixed on Alice.

She felt the intensity of the spirit's glare.

'What… what do you want?' said Alice. She knew what she must do, she must go forward into the ghost's aura, to see if she could use her mysterious power to connect with it. And yet – yet – the prospect was so awful, so terrifying, she stayed put.

The woman stood and walked swiftly towards her in her ragged dress. Her mouth opened, black in between those foul teeth with their roots exposed, as if to speak – or perhaps bite. Alice stumbled back on to the small landing, her hand going out instinctively to the banister to stop herself falling down the stairs.

'Stay back!' she said, putting up her other hand to protect herself.

But the woman's eyes were fierce amidst the lost flesh and she reached out as if to grab her and then, because she could retreat no further, Alice found herself immersed within the creature's aura…

58.

It is a five mile walk back from the mill and she is aching all over, a fever caught from Betty Norris, she is sure, the slattern was spluttering all day amidst the fluff. But she can't miss a day's work and a day's fine so will have to return tomorrow, no matter what. She has a little feverfew left on her shelf and will take it in a pot of boiled water when she is back. She shakes and clutches her sides on the path that snakes across the moor. It would all have been so different, had Carmichael survived the war with the Boers.

She is lost in her thoughts of her soldier husband, a private in the Fusiliers, when someone calls her name from the autumn's emptiness:

'Gretel!'

She starts and looks up, sees the man Clay up ahead. Still in black with his Reverend's collar, despite the rumours the Bishop is on the verge of removing him from his post for his sins.

'What do you want?' she says, seeing him striding down the path towards her.

'Nothing,' he says, drawing near. 'Nothing.'

'Out my way, then.' She says it with all the authority she can muster from her Teutonic accent.

He stands in front of her. She stops, he is tall.

'You have a pretty face,' he says.

He has been at her many times before, pressing her for attention. Unable to continue on the path, she steps sideways into the heather. He reaches out and grabs her wrist.

'You're all the same, you men of the cloth,' she hisses. She remembers the tales of Reverend Wallace from Edale, what he did to those boys. May he roast forever in hellfire.

'Yes, a very pretty face,' he says, ignoring her. 'I think I will have it…'

With a sense of fatality drawn from her illness and exhaustion, she realises this is a moment of greater significance for her life than she would ever have expected on a dreary Tuesday night. She sees him reach for something in his belt, a knife, a knife with a leather-wrapped handle and a silvery, asymmetrical pommel…

She attempts one last shake of her arm to break free, but his grip is firm.

59.

Alice could scarcely breathe, her mouth full of crumpled linen.

Somehow, she was facedown on the bed, sucking in darkness, her soul lost to another woman's sudden terror. She must have staggered forward and fallen on the bed when the ghost vanished, the vision faded. Her thoughts were a torrent like the storm on the night before, her feelings a broken dam.

Gretel, grackle. A boy fishing for a more familiar word to describe the chaotic entity encroaching on his life.

A poor widow, a Victorian woman alone, no wife nor mother nor housekeeper. German – or rather Prussian, in all likelihood, at that time – and therefore even more on the outskirts of society.

Preyed upon.

I think I will have it. Her pretty face. Surely not…

Alice couldn't stomach it. Not that thought. Like a spark in the eye, her mind faltered at the terrible connection. The Devil in the basement, the Devil in the cave. The sunken eyes, the high, swollen cheeks, as if he was…

Wearing another face.

A woman's face.

The Grackle's face. *Gretel's* face.

He was not the Devil. He was just a man. A ghost of a man in a twisted, fashioned suit, with a woman's face.

Although if he could do such a thing to a poor woman, might he not deserve the title?

Sheepy

60.

The boy woke later than normal.

He could tell because there was already a greyness around the edge of his curtains, the starting of daylight. He checked his alarm clock. 7:08.

He yawned and yawned again, pushing his arms wide out into the air, half-twisting under the blankets. Then leaned over and switched on his light. He needed the toilet desperately and swung himself out of bed.

When he came back into his room, he thought he would read his book a while before breakfast. He sauntered up to the curtains in his slippers and pulled them open. Outside was drained of colour, the fruit tree, walls, moors bleached cold and damp by the coming winter. The boy felt his heart sink. What he really needed was…

'Sheepy!'

He shouted the word out loud. His cuddly companion was there, sitting on its backside, chin on belly, a short distance up the hill from the garden. His eyesight was excellent, kept sharp by spotting birds high over the moors. He was sure it was Sheepy, he could tell by the flop of the head, hopeless but eternally loveable, the overblown ears sagging around his snout.

How did he get there? He must have dropped him when he was with Alice, coming back across the moors from her house. In the back of his mind was an image of the radiator, a memory of perching Sheepy on top of it, but he knew now that memory was wrong. Sheepy had fallen from his pack before they'd reached the gate. Poor Sheepy! He must be soaked and dirty and completely unloved.

Knocking about the room, the boy tugged on his clothes, his jeans, sweatshirt, and trainers, then thundered down through the house, without even thinking to look in on his grandad as he went past. At the back door, he pulled his duffle coat off the hook and slipped it on, then twisted the key in the lock and ran outside.

He ran straight to the gate, splashing in wet grass as he ignored the delicate curve of the flagstone path. He yanked open the gate and looked up towards where he had seen the sheep.

Sheepy was gone!

The boy's breath stopped in his chest as he stared around. He blinked in panic.

No, there he was! A bit further up than he'd thought, near a clutch of hawthorn on the trail heading off along the hillside. How could he have got that wrong? Angles, of course. The angle of his bedroom window to the path, something like that. But at least Sheepy was there, he was right…

Ben ran as fast as he could up the slope, cutting off a corner of the path to get there quicker, stumbling on clumps of grass and keeping himself up by the force of will alone. He had found Sheepy!

Moments later, he was a few steps away from the cuddly toy, panting but relieved. He could see Sheepy was muddy and bedraggled, in the shade of the hawthorns. But now all doubt was gone, it was his sheep.

But as he was coming up to Sheepy, as his hands reached out, a shape stepped out from the scrub in front of him, blocking his way.

The boy jerked to a halt and looked up.

There was a man standing there, a solid giant of a man, with glasses and a rock band T-shirt.

'Hello,' said the man, his voice deep, his accent from further north.

The boy was so intent on his sheep that instead of replying he tried to reach around the side of the man to pick it up. The man caught him around the tops of his arms and lifted him easily off his feet into the air. With a second decisive move he had the boy pinned against his side.

'Put me down!' shouted the boy, stretching his free arm out towards Sheepy.

And then, as he struggled to wrest himself away from the man, the boy became aware of a second figure, a woman with black hair, emerging from behind the scrub. The woman was pulling open a large bag, a hessian sack, as she came towards him.

Ben started screaming. The last thing he saw as his head swivelled round was the flash of one-half of the sun, perched on the ridge of the hill above them.

Vult Scire

61.

Aitor arrived shortly after midday.

As soon as she heard the crunch of the tyres on the gravel drive, Alice leapt up. The bright yellow of his car, a small Renault, was a vibrant challenge to the drab moorland behind it. It felt like... the arrival of the cavalry.

She flung open the door and ran out to greet him.

'Alice!' he was out of the car before she even reached him, opening his arms to receive her.

'Thank you, thank you for coming,' she said. He was a short man, not much taller than her, but still she managed to hold her face against his shoulder, to bask in his solidity.

'No problems, darling, always,' he said, rubbing her back. 'Aitor is always here for you.'

They pulled back, holding arms and looking at each other. Alice took in his bleached hair, the ear stud, his bright brown eyes. The five o'clock shadow of stubble. She felt her eyes stinging with relief. Aitor let go of her and thumbed away the tears.

'You've been having a hard time, Alice,' he said, 'Again.'

Alice nodded. Hearing his mellifluous accent reassured her.

'Let's go inside,' she said. 'I need to tell you about last night.'

'Something else happened?' he said.

'Yes.'

He reached back into the car, grabbed his bag, then slammed the door and followed her into the house.

62.

'Shit… *bastardo*…'

Aitor sat back in the chair, wiping his mouth with his hand. 'The Reverend cut her face off – it's him you saw in the basement at the Rectory! How you described him to me – the sunken eyes, the swollen, seemingly rotten flesh – he was *wearing* her face!'

'That's exactly what I thought, Aitor,' said Alice. A weight was lifting from her as they talked, sitting across from each other drinking coffee at Victor's white breakfast table.

'This is very troubling, Alice,' he said. 'The poor woman.'

'Yes. And Aitor, last night makes me think Gretel must have found out about my ability by visiting me here, in Victor's cottage. I have these vague memories of waking in the night before Ben turned up. Of sensing someone – but they're dim…'

'Yes, that makes sense,' said Aitor. 'The cottage must be in her ghostly trajectory. Maybe she sensed your power just by observing you – and then sent Ben to get you?'

Alice shrugged. 'Yes, I guess so.' She wasn't sure she liked the idea of ghosts sensing her ability. She imagined it as a beacon to them, attracting them from all around. It made her shiver.

'I've been thinking about Clay all night,' she said hurriedly, trying to take her mind off it. 'He must have been completely corrupt, evil…'

'I did a little search last night, too,' said Aitor.

'Your poor mum!' Alice said. 'I feel so guilty…'

'She's fine. She was watching Squid Games on Netflix with a bottle of brandy.'

Alice shook her head. 'What did you find?'

'There's not much on the normal web. Horace Clay was the Reverend at St Barnabas here from 1879 to 1883. He was the middle of three brothers from a wealthy Derbyshire family, who made their money from the charcoal industry. Went to Keble college, Oxford to study Theology – one of the first students there, it was quite new then. There are a few items about his passion for Jackson's Rocks and how he developed the amphitheatre and Clay's Chamber, how it became a tourist attraction. You can even find mention of those on the Peak tourist website. And then there are one or two that mention his turn to occultism and the unsavoury events that started happening – the death of the boy, the disappearance of two local women. The man who said he saw the Devil up there. Clay set up a group along the lines of the infamous Hellfire club…'

'Douglas mentioned that to me,' said Alice.

'Yes, the secret society for the elite, started in the eighteenth century. They met to get up to no good, to transgress social norms. Clay's group was called *Vult Scire.*'

'Latin,' said Alice.

'Smart lady,' said Aitor, grinning.

'Something like, he wants to know?' she said, trying to remember her school days.

'Yes. Or just 'Want to Know', or maybe 'The Will to Know'.'

Alice smiled, pleased with herself.

'And then there's some record of his fall from grace, the Bishop getting rid of him, and his suicide. But little else, and very little detail, I'm afraid.'

Alice frowned. 'Damn,' she muttered.

'However…' said Aitor, grinning.

'What?' she said eagerly.

'I also looked through some of the dark web forums I keep an eye on last night, and I did find something interesting. *Very* interesting…'

'What's that?'

Aitor pulled his smart, rose gold MacBook from his canvas pack and set it on the table.

'I'll show you,' he said, lifting the screen and starting to type in the address bar.

'The dark web is something you hear about all the time,' said Alice. 'But I'm not even sure I know what it is…'

'Just a way for people to share stuff – mostly malicious – anonymously,' said Aitor, concentrating on the screen. 'No digital footprint – or at least, no standard footprint.'

'So it's used by criminals?'

'Yes. But also some who wouldn't survive if their government knew what they were up to.'

Alice watched a series of suggested domains appear in the dropdown bar. Aitor selected one – she fleetingly noticed the word *tor* in there – and clicked it.

The *This site can't be reached* message appeared.

'Shhh…it,' said Aitor.

'What is it?'

'It's gone down already.'

'What do you mean?'

'There was a discussion forum here yesterday. But it's been taken down.'

'Who by?'

Aitor shrugged. 'Probably the owners. But it could have been Google, Amazon – or the government. Or it might have had a Snapchat-style, disappear-after-a-certain-period code.'

'What was on it?'

Aitor opened Finder. 'I'll show you – at least a snippet.'

He opened a file.

'Took a screenshot of some of it,' he said. 'You never know when something like this is going to happen.'

Alice looked at the section, which was a conversation between three – no four – individuals, identified by their circular avatars with no names.

Eye avatar: *this is big we're coming*

Squiggle through a white disc avatar: *please come*

Ram's horns: *There's a psychometrist. He's supposed to be the best, and he's interested.*

Squiggle: *very interested!*

Black orb with stars: *if it's him it's straight away no pissing about*

Horns: *No point delaying, anything might happen with a kid.*

Eye: *on the rocks?*

Squiggle: *maybe, or the home.*

Horns: *We owe a lot to the lady.*

Squiggle: *serendipity*

Horns: *More than that we hope.*
Eye: *vult scire*
Horns: *Vult Scire*

'Wow,' said Alice. 'Just… wow. Vult Scire – Clay's group,' said Alice.

'Chances are.'

'And the mention of the rocks…'

'Jackson's Rocks?' said Aitor.

'We could do with more,' she said.

'Shame they took it down.'

'Since last night and this morning?'

'Yes.'

'What's the forum called?'

'Moments on the Earth.'

'Doesn't sound very ominous. How come you found it?'

'I'm always delving into these anonymous forums. Some have a lot of information about the occult. I checked a few dozen threads last night and this one leapt out, for obvious reasons.'

Alice reread it. 'They're clearly very excited about something,' she said. 'What is a psychometrist, anyway?'

'Someone who senses the history of objects through touch,' said Aitor.

'Like telepathy or telekinesis?' said Alice.

'Yes. And ESP. The psychic powers.'

'Alleged powers.' Alice thought of all the horror films she'd watched, the novels she'd read. 'I don't know where to draw the line anymore,' she said.

'Join the club.'

Alice looked at him. 'I think we should go back to the Rectory,' she said. She fished her phone from her pocket and checked it. 'I'm surprised they haven't called me…'

'Now?' said Aitor.

Alice nodded.

'OK,' said Aitor. 'And Alice…'

'Yes?'

'One more thing to think about…'

'What's that?'

'You know what tonight is, don't you?'

Alice frowned. An image of a half-cut pumpkin, a work-in-progress, sitting on the Rectory kitchen table flashed in her mind.

'Yes,' she said. 'Halloween. But surely that doesn't mean anything?'

'When the seal between this and the spirit world is weakest,' said Aitor.

'Oh,' said Alice.

63.

The drive to the Rectory was absurdly convoluted considering it was less than three miles away. The B road at the bottom of the drive up to Victor's cottage wound deep into the valley before finally veering back up to a junction with a minor road signposted to Tiss. After a couple of minutes on this they passed a hand painted sign on a wall indicating the drive to Bracken Hill Farm.

Alice dipped her head at the sign as they passed it. 'There it is, Bracken Hill,' she said. She was feeling a little car sick with the way Aitor did everything so hurriedly, both driving and speaking. 'The one Douglas said was a sweetener to get a local contract – fund a group of conservationists as part of your CSR.'

'Corporate Social Responsibility?' Aitor snorted. 'Not so, darling!'

'What?'

'I checked out the details,' he said, as he revved the little car away around a bend. 'Peaks Water doesn't own it. But it is owned by one of their staff.'

'Who's that?'

'Their Chief Finance Officer. Melissa something, I've forgotten now. She's a big lover of the outdoors, according to her profile on their website.'

'Douglas was wrong?' said Alice.

Aitor shrugged, watching the road. 'Looks like it.'

'Strange,' said Alice. 'Maybe she set it up as a conservation centre on her own. We need to check them out later. That Archie Jones, he…'

'What?'

'Freaked me out.'

Aitor thought for a moment. 'Why?'

'He was over presumptuous. Don't get me wrong, in some ways he was deferential. But even that was like overcompensation. It was as if…'

'Go on…'

'As if he thought he had the right to know me. To get inside me, even though I'd only just met him.'

Aitor pulled a face. 'I think we should check out this Mr Jones,' he said, as he switched down gears for another curve in the road he took – at least in Alice's eyes – far too quickly.

64

'Wow – some vicarage!'

Aitor arched his back to look up at the impressive Victorian façade. 'But definitely in need of a little love and attention – especially a roofer.'

Alice followed his gaze and saw some of the slate tiles were loose and one or two had even fallen off. She nodded.

'And you say he bought it when he retired because they were getting rid of it?' Aitor continued. 'They obviously pay priests more here than they do back home!'

'Yes, I was surprised,' said Alice. 'He had an income from writing, too, I think. And I guess he must have inherited the money when Ben's parents died.'

'That would explain it,' said Aitor, nodding.

Alice rapped the door knocker, then stepped back and looked up at the second floor windows, at Douglas's room on the left.

'His curtains are closed,' she said. 'He sleeps heavily with his illness. And if Ben's in his bedroom…'

She rapped the knocker again, the sound echoing faintly in the valley around them.

'Round the back?' Aitor suggested.

'Yes. I suppose so.'

They headed down the side of the building and found themselves up against a head-high garden gate. Aitor lifted the latch and pushed but it held near the top.

'There's a bolt,' he said, reaching over the top. He paused and looked around the side passage. 'That'll do,' he said, stooping down and tipping the black water from a large terracotta pot. He turned it upside down, then stepped up on to it.

'Perfect,' he said, reaching over and sliding back the bolt. He stepped down and opened the gate. They went through to the back garden.

'We left the back door open last night by accident,' said Alice. She walked up and tried the handle. 'I can't believe it,' she said, as the door swung open. 'You'd think he'd have learnt his lesson…'

She leaned into the kitchen. 'Hello?' she called. The house was silent, except for the solid ticking of the clock above the door. 'Anyone in?' she called more loudly. 'It's me, Alice!'

She turned back to Aitor, standing in his orange puffer jacket behind her. 'Come on,' she said, stepping on to the doormat and scuffing the soles of her trainers. She walked in, shouting 'Hello!' again. Aitor followed.

'Douglas – Ben!' Alice called, walking down the hall, checking the cellar door, which was firmly shut. 'Anyone here?'

Aitor peered round the doors of the study and living room as she went to the foot of the stairs and looked up.

'Douglas? There's something wrong…' she said, as Aitor peered into the dining room. She leapt up the stairs, two at a time, reached the landing and headed straight to Douglas's room. The door was ajar. With an increasing sense of alarm, she shoved it open.

'Oh God!' she cried. 'Aitor!'

65.

She knew as soon as she saw him that he was dead.

The curtains had not been drawn properly, so a shaft of light stretched across the carpet to highlight the grim expression of the man lying in the bed. As she hurried to his side, her first senseless thought was she was staring at a skull. His eyes were rolled back into his head, showing yellowed whites. His skin was thin and drawn, the colour of curdled cream. His jaw hung open, showing his discoloured teeth and a bulge of greyish tongue. The poor man looked horrendous, Alice thought, like…

Like he died screaming.

Before she could move, Aitor was at Douglas's side, stooping down, doing the sensible things you were supposed to do to see if he was alive, whilst Alice, knowing the truth, stood there immobile, her fingers across her mouth, her brain a collapsing vacuum.

'Call 999,' said Aitor.

'Ben…' said Alice. She turned and ran out, down the landing towards the boy's room.

66.

Clutching the door handle, Alice gaped at the empty room.

The bird drawings, the unmade bed, the table lamp still on, the guidebook lit by its soft light.

'Ben!' she shouted. Instinctively, she dropped to her hands and knees and peered under the bed. Then she ran to the window and looked out in the garden. The back gate, the one linking to the moorland path, was open. Her head moved sharply as she looked at all the places he might be, hidden behind the glass house, a flash of green coat in the bushes, somewhere up on the windswept grass of the moor…

Nowhere. He was nowhere.

Alice ran to the room where she'd slept, the bathroom, even clicking open the door of the linen cupboard, shouting *Ben* as she darted about.

'Alice – we need an ambulance!' shouted Aitor.

'Aitor, you call them! I need to find Ben.'

Aitor was at Douglas's door, his usually cheerful face grim and slightly bewildered. 'He's stone-cold dead,' he said, pulling his phone out of his jacket and starting to dial. 'I'll help search while I'm calling,' he added, following Alice downstairs.

She ran into the dining room, glancing around at the drab, patchily stained table and chairs, the Welsh dresser crammed with old-fashioned crockery and china animals. She came out, joined Aitor in a more thorough check of the lounge.

'Where is he… where is he…?' After a glance into the study, she turned to Aitor who was now talking to the emergency services.

'I'm going down the cellar,' she mouthed, reaching for the door handle.

Aitor placed his hand over the phone. 'I'll come,' he said, then lifting his hand, said: 'Yes, the Rectory, it's on the edge of the village of Tiss, I don't know the street name or postcode, no, sorry…'

Alice opened the door and, feeling a cold clutch at her heart, hurried down the stairs, followed closely by her friend.

'I can't come any further, Alice, the signal's breaking up,' said Aitor. 'I need to go back up!'

At the bottom of the steps, Alice stopped. She looked up at him, framed in the glare of the open door.

'OK,' she said. 'I'm fine.'

She watched as he retraced his steps to the top, began talking again to the emergency services.

'Yes, no problems, I can say it again – Aitor Elizondo – E.L.I.Z.O.N.D.O. – yes, Aitor – A.I.T.O.R. – and I'm here with Alice Deaton, who is… a friend of his. Yes, I…'

Alice lost the thread of what he was saying as her attention turned to the opening in the wall and the cold cellar beyond.

'Ben!' she shouted, moving more slowly now. She flicked on the lights but was still overpowered by the place. Images of the looming Devil, his grisly face, of the scrubbed pentagram, flashed through her mind.

'Ben?'

She walked into the main basement, passed a black sewing machine on a bench, reached the table over the magic circle, saw the cable reel and Tiddlywinks, green and blue and red and yellow plastic counters which, when she looked away, seemed to flash into a shape at the corner of her eye, the pentagram again – but as soon as she looked back were just a random scatter. There was something deeply bad, wrong, about this place, the memory of that man, of what he had done to those women and…

Who had drawn that circle, chalked out those runes? Who was it?

Horribly, she felt she knew.

Who else could it be?

68.

'He's not there,' she said, returning to Aitor in the kitchen.

'Shit,' he whispered.

'Is the ambulance coming?'

'Yes, but they aren't close. Half an hour minimum.'

'I think we need the police too.'

'They're coming, because the death was unexpected and there's no obvious next of kin.'

'We're going to have to report Ben missing.'

'Yes, I told them about him, too,' said Aitor. 'Is there anywhere you think he might have gone?'

She shook her head despairingly. 'I don't know. He didn't mention any friends in the village but surely he must have one or two? Or maybe my house again?'

Aitor sucked in air through his teeth. 'Did he have your number?'

'I gave it to Douglas before I left.'

'Sent it to his phone?'

'No – he didn't have a mobile, so I wrote it down.'

They went and looked at the telephone table, a small pad beside it, but it wasn't there.

'Ben might not have been able to find it – if it was you he thought of going to,' said Aitor.

'Yes. We ought to get back, to check…'

'We have to wait for the police, let them know what we're doing.'

Alice raked her hand through her hair.

69.

She stood in the bay window of the dining room, fidgeting and sipping water and watching the police car, a marked-up BMW, lunging up the pitted drive to park alongside the ambulance.

Two officers, a man and woman bulked up in stab vests, climbed out of the car and approached the house, sizing it up. The woman spotted Alice, who waved at her and went through to the hall to open the door.

At the threshold, the man checked his notepad and looked up at her: 'Ms. Deaton?'

'Yes.'

'I'm PC Davis, this is my colleague, PC Grint. I think it was your friend –' again he checked his pad, '– Mr Elizondo, who made the call?'

'That's right. They're all upstairs. With Douglas.'

'May we?'

She led them up the stairs, in silence, then along the landing to the old priest's room where the paramedics, watched by Aitor, were standing over Douglas's body, still twisted amid the bedcovers.

Alice noticed the look that passed between the officers when they saw the old man's face.

'When was the last time you saw him?'

'Yesterday morning. I left the house around half past ten.'

After speaking to the paramedics, PC Davis had called in a Crime Scene Investigator ('just to be on the safe side' Alice heard him say quietly), then the two officers had taken her and Aitor down to the kitchen where they were now sitting. PC Grint, a young woman with ginger hair and a small, reddish birthmark at the corner of her mouth, was leading the questioning.

'And you say you met him… how again? He came over to your house across the moor? Is that right?'

'Yes.' Alice glanced at Aitor, who was sitting chewing his thumb nail at the end of the table. She saw him stop himself from pulling a face, aware of how it would look in front of the officers. What should she say?

'In that storm?'

'Yes. He said his grandad was ill, and he needed help.'

The police officers looked at each other. 'Why didn't he call for help? He didn't know you, did he?'

'No, as I've said, we'd never met. I don't know why he didn't call someone else. Maybe, I don't know, maybe calling the police felt too much for him.'

'It takes a bit of confidence to pick up the phone and dial 999,' said Aitor. 'Especially for a kid.'

PC Grint looked at him carefully. 'Yes,' she said. 'So he walked – what, over two miles? – to you?'

Alice laughed anxiously. 'I don't know why he came all that way. I guess it would have been quicker to have gone into the village.'

'Yes. Much quicker. Do you know if he has any friends in the village?'

'I don't, sorry.'

'Isn't there an old farm in between here and your place?' said PC Davis, tall and chiselled, with a deep Scottish accent.

'Er – there is,' said Alice. 'It's a bit off the route. Down in the valley.'

'Wonder why he didn't stop there?'

Alice shrugged. 'I really don't…'

'No worries,' said PC Grint. 'But you came with him, through the storm, and spoke to his grandad. And then stayed the night out of concern for them but left the next morning.'

'Yes.'

'OK.' Again, the woman glanced at her colleague. She huffed. 'Well, the important thing now is not to lose any more time – we need to get looking for Ben.'

'You can do that straight away?' said Aitor.

'Given the circumstances,' said PC Grint.

'That's good,' said Alice.

'Can you call a Misper in?' said the policewoman.

PC Davis nodded, stood up and headed off down the hall. Alice heard him go out the front door.

'OK,' said PC Grint, standing up. 'You say you've checked the house thoroughly?'

'Yes,' said Alice.

'Well, I'm going to have another look round, to make sure,' said the woman. 'Then, when my colleague's back, we'll work out our initial search.'

Alice glanced at Aitor.

'We can check the garden,' he said.

'Yes, don't go too far,' said PC Grint.

Alice felt a shiver of paranoia. Did they suspect her?

71.

PC Davis came out into the garden, where Aitor and Alice had just completed their search.

'They're sending a couple of cars over to help look for him,' he said. He looked up at the heavy clouds above the moor. 'Let's hope he's not up there somewhere.'

Alice was feeling increasingly uneasy. 'Can you get a helicopter?' she said.

The policeman grimaced. 'There's one in Derby,' he said. 'I suspect control might dispatch it soon. If he doesn't turn up.'

'I think there's something strange going on here,' said Alice, decisively. The wind blew her hair across her face and she pushed it back.

'Why's that?' said the policeman.

'I found a… a kind of pentagram, down in the cellar,' she said.

'Pentagram?'

'Yes. You know. Sort of… an occult thing.'

'Oh. Perhaps we should take a look.'

'I'm afraid I… scrubbed it off.'

'Why?'

'I thought it was a bit sick. I realise now I shouldn't have.'

'Do you know who might have done it?'

'No,' said Alice, adding quickly: 'And, in case I forget, someone came to the door, yesterday morning, before I left.'

'Who?'

The policeman looked concerned. Alice realised she should have said straight away. 'A man. His name was Archibald Jones. He said he was looking for Bracken Hill Farm.'

'Where?'

'It's the farm you mentioned earlier. In between here and my – my boss's – house.'

'It's a conservation centre now,' said Aitor.

'And what did he do?'

'Well – he talked quite a bit – nothing significant. I gave him directions and he went off,' said Alice. 'But I saw him again, when I was walking home. He had come across the conservation volunteers enroute and started working with them. They were clearing scrub at Jackson's Rocks.'

'Right,' said the man. 'Sounds innocent enough. Why are you concerned?'

'I don't know. He was just a bit… odd.'

'How?'

'Intense.'

'OK. We'll get someone to go and speak to them.'

'Can we go home now and check my place? Ben might have gone there,' said Alice. As soon as she said it, she realised what a stupid question it was. She was a free woman, after all.

The policeman appeared to think. 'We've got your mobile numbers, haven't we?' he said.

Alice and Aitor nodded.

'There's sure to be more we need to talk to you about.'

72

There was no one at the cottage when they got back.

'We've got to get out there, keep looking,' said Alice, noticing the increasing gloom outside the kitchen window.

'Sit down, Alice,' said Aitor. 'Much better for us to think first. Ben could be anywhere. Anywhere at all. But we – more importantly, you – know things. And if we think it through, we may have a chance of finding him. A chance that maybe the police and search parties don't have.'

Alice nodded, took a seat at the breakfast bar opposite him.

'OK, a boy comes to find you because a ghost, a mutilated woman, has told him to,' said Aitor. 'She says you can help him. You go with him to his house and meet his grandad, who the boy says is being slowly drained by visitations from the Devil.'

His logic was good, but still every squiggle of feeling told her to get out there, to look, search hard, before the night closed everything down.

'Did Ben say anything about this ghost – the Grackle, who you think is Gretel – telling him you could help *just* him? Or did he say she wanted you to help his grandad too?'

Alice thought. 'No. He said something strange. He said she didn't like him – his grandad – and it was only him she was protecting, Ben. And when I spoke to Douglas about her, he said she was a bad creature, and suspected she might have got Ben to bring me there to do *me* harm.'

'Hmm,' said Aitor. 'That puts a different slant on things. OK, setting that aside for the moment, whilst you're there, Douglas tells you about this Victorian priest, Horace Clay, who became an occultist. You see the Devil in the basement and have one of your *experiences* with him, in which you see him kill a woman in the caves at Jackson's Rocks.'

Alice nodded, trying to block the shocking memory from refreshing in her mind. 'In Clay's Chamber…' she muttered.

'Sorry,' said Aitor. 'Think of yourself in a diving bell, there's a mighty wall of metal and pressure-proof glass protecting you from the image, from its harm.'

'Mmm. Go on,' she said, looking at the half-eaten cheese sandwich on her plate. She couldn't eat more.

'You find a pentagram on the floor, drawn with chalk, with curious symbols. Also, while you're there, the boy's sheep toy disappears. The door is unlocked and you suspect someone might have come in and taken it.'

'Yes,' said Alice.

'And the next morning a man knocks looking for Bracken Hill Farm conservation centre. You send him on his way, but don't trust him. Nor the other conservationists when you meet them a little later, after you've had another unpleasant experience on the Rocks.'

'Finally, last night the Grackle visits you *here*. From your strange ability to feel what ghosts feel – *you* possessing *them* – you realise she was probably mutilated and killed by Horace Clay.'

'Bastard.' Alice shut her eyes.

'Yes.'

'Where does all that lead us?' said Alice.

Aitor leaned over his plate and took a big bite of his sandwich. He chewed it twice and swallowed, then gulped down some juice.

'There's one big thing here,' he said, taking another bite. 'I think it might hold the key.'

'What?'

'We know some people – only a small fraction of the population, you and I included – can see ghosts.'

'Yes.'

'And you – uniquely – have the gift to see inside them, to find out what is keeping them back, the pain or guilt or whatever it is that stops them being released to the other side. The thing that stops them crossing over.'

'Gift?' said Alice. 'Feels more like a burden.'

'But from what you've told me, Ben has something else altogether. Something unique too.'

'Of course,' said Alice quietly, realising the significance at last. 'He can *talk* to them…'

73.

'Exactly,' said Aitor, his eyes shining. 'Ben can talk to spirits. Not like some hokum psychic. He can *really* talk to them.'

'Amazing,' said Alice. 'What an amazing power.' She stood up and, flipping the lid of the food bin, tossed the remains of her sandwich in. 'But how does that help us find him?'

'I'm still thinking,' said Aitor, pressing his hands together over his lips. 'OK, let's imagine. Say that there's an active local occultist, or group of occultists, who have come here because of the legend of the corrupt

Reverend, Horace Clay. Perhaps taking on the name of his group, Vult Scire.'

'Or it's the same group that never shut down?' said Alice.

'Possibly,' Aitor mused. 'Let's assume they are the ones who have drawn the pentagram in the cellar, because they want to summon him for a particular ritual.'

'Can you summon ghosts?' said Alice. 'I thought that was demons?'

Aitor shrugged. 'That's what séances are supposed to be about.'

'Oh yes,' said Alice, feeling foolish.

'So maybe this is just an elaborate séance. They want to call Clay back…'

'And that's why they want Ben! To speak with him…' Alice said. She gasped. 'But…'

Aitor put his elbows on the table and pressed his hands together beneath his chin. His eyes blazed. 'Oh Alice…' he whispered.

'What is it?'

'Vult Scire!'

Alice thought. 'They want to know?' she said.

'Exactly!' said Aitor. 'What does every secret society that's *ever* existed want? To know! Not the stuff anyone can find on Wikipedia, or by sitting around thinking all day. They want *hidden* knowledge! It makes them feel special. Elite, elect, anointed, chosen.'

'And the greatest hidden knowledge…' began Alice.

'The thing every human has struggled with since the dawn of time is…' said Aitor.

'What happens to us when we die.'

74

'Exactly – they want to know what the afterlife is really like!'

'And Ben holds the key,' said Alice.

'Precisely. If they can get the ghost and Ben in the same place at the same time they can use him to talk to the ghost. For the first time ever, in the *whole* history of humanity…'

'They can find out what it's like on the other side of the veil!' Alice thought for a moment. 'But what about Mediums, or whatever they're called? Like you just said about the seances - isn't that what they do?'

'To an extent, yes, they supposedly channel the dead,' said Aitor. 'But, whilst I've found lots of evidence of ghosts – and, of course, seen them myself – I've never found a Spirit Medium I'm completely convinced by. Most of them are shams. A few can probably do what they say they can, but I don't think they communicate in a proper, two-way fashion like Ben can.'

Alice felt giddy. She thought about that old-fashioned word, swooning. She felt like she was swooning.

'Imagine it,' said Aitor, his dark eyes gleaming. 'The ultimate knowledge. The members of Vult Scire *know* ghosts are real, can appear here on earth. But they have no idea what it is like for them, in the afterlife. What might they be able to do with that knowledge?

'Perhaps they're scared of dying,' she said.

'Aren't we all?' said Aitor. Then: 'I think you have it though. Like those aristocrats in the Hellfire Club and other secret societies, they can't stand the thought of their own demise. Their own annihilation. And if there's any mechanism at all to be discovered that can keep them going, they'll use it, regardless of the consequences.'

Alice thought of Eloise Bossuyt, the pact she'd made to stay around after she died.

'Think of all those billionaires having their heads cryogenically frozen. They're scared. They're petrified of dying. And these people are too!'

'They'd probably rather even become a ghost than be obliterated,' said Alice.

Aitor puffed. 'I wouldn't be surprised. But from all this, regardless of their own mortality, they have the faintest chance – but still, the best chance ever – of finding out what happens next. It's the ultimate goal of every occultist who ever lived.'

'Even if it turns out to be a hard pill to swallow.'

'Vult Scire – the clue's in the name. They just want to know.'

'OK,' said Alice. 'All mindboggling. But – supposing this is all good conjecture, where does it put us now?'

They were interrupted by the crashing drums of a David Bowie song, Alice's ringtone. She picked her phone off the counter.

'Hello,' she said.

'Ms Deaton?'

'Yes.'

'I'm Detective Inspector Tutt, I'm leading the search for the missing boy you told us about, Ben Davis. I wanted to give you a quick update on what's been happening.' His voice was hoarse, she imagined how much he must have been talking throughout the day. 'Our officers have door knocked the village but nothing. We also sent a search party with dogs out on the moor. They found a trail behind the garden but it was weak and disappeared a short distance from the house. We suspect it might have been a residual scent from when he walked over the moors with you on Thursday. That was right, wasn't it, it was Thursday?'

'Yes,' she said.

'A helicopter's going out from Derby shortly. I'm guessing you haven't found anything of interest?'

Alice looked at Aitor. 'No…' she said. 'No.' What could she tell him?

He was silent for a moment, as if waiting.

'Where are you now?' he said finally.

'Home.'

'I assume there was no sign of him having been there?'

'No,' she said. 'None at all. Did you check the farm?'

'Bracken Hill? Yes, one of our officers went round, spoke to them. There was nothing of note.'

Alice huffed. 'OK,' she said. 'Have you searched the Rocks, too?'

'Yes, the dogs went all over,' he said. 'But – nothing.'

'Is there anything at all we can do?' she said.

'Not now,' said the detective. 'Stay there. There's still a chance he's got a little freaked out by his grandad dying. If he's going to come back, he might well come to you, as you're one of the only people he knows.'

'Right,' said Alice.

'Just wait, Ms Deaton,' said the policeman. 'We'll call you if anything else comes up.'

75

After the call, they both sat there, Aitor clutching his cheeks, elbows on the table, Alice sliding a thumb thoughtlessly over the screen of her phone.

'Supposing… supposing he headed out there, out the back, on to the moors, for some reason?' said Alice.

'He would have called the police, surely,' said Aitor. 'He doesn't sound like a foolish boy.'

'Maybe he was confused,' said Alice. 'Perhaps he was coming to find me, to tell me Douglas was dead? Maybe the Grackle sent him again?'

'But the dogs lost his scent on the path.'

'The detective thought it was an old trail from two days before.'

'Maybe it wasn't?' said Aitor.

'How do you mean?'

'Maybe – oh, I don't know – maybe he was stopped by someone?'

Alice's heartbeat quickened. Her mouth went dry. 'They've taken him,' she said.

'I don't know, Alice…'

'Aitor, they've taken him. It all adds up. We have to go to the farm ourselves. To see if he's there.'

'Let's call the police about it.'

'They've already been. They won't be able to search it, they'll get caught up with a warrant. But we won't. We owe it to him. We've got to do everything we can. We might be completely wrong – but we might be right! And unless we go there, now, we'll never know. And, if we don't…'

'What?'

'We might be too late.' An image flashed in her mind, of the partially cut pumpkin on the Rectory kitchen table. A chill gripped her spine. 'Aitor – it's Halloween tonight! Like you said, the seal between this and the other world is supposed to be at its weakest, isn't it?'

Aitor wrinkled his nose. 'Maybe, Alice, but…'

'It might be just hokum. But if they're trying to summon the Devil – Clay – they'll want to maximise all their chances, won't they?'

Aitor shook his head slowly, thinking.

'Who knows what they might do to him?' said Alice.

Bracken Hill Farm

76.

There was an orange ice warning on the dashboard and the temperature showed 3°.

They drove through the black night, headlights picking out the jagged stones in the walls, the grey-and-black fleck of the road. The rain was intermittent, silver swept away by the occasional hefty clunk of the wipers. Most of the time, they sat in silence.

It didn't take long to get back to the vicinity of the farm. When the wall ended on their left for a wide gate, Aitor pulled over and stopped the car. They sat there, hearing the tick of the engine, the muted press of the wind at the gaps in the car's armour.

'It might be nothing,' said Alice, suddenly fazed. Inside, it felt like she was imploding with anxiety and doubt.

'Come on,' said Aitor. 'We're here now.'

Alice stared ahead into the darkness. 'We look. Just look in the windows…'

'Sure,' said Aitor, swallowing.

They used their phone torches, pointed at the ground, as they made their way down the road to the farm drive. Alice was grateful her pompom hat was keeping her ears warm as leaves swept into the torchlight.

They came to the entrance of the drive and stopped.

'It should be easier to make our way without light from here,' said Alice.

Aitor gave a small nod and they switched off their torches. Alice felt overwhelmed by the blackness, like a physical pressure on her eyes. She took a slight step back to steady herself and knocked against Aitor's arm.

'Alright,' he said. 'Let your eyes accustom.'

The noise of the night became dominant. Alice heard the wind pushing through withered leaves, a susurration that was somehow not gentle, more resistant to the enforced change of bad weather, of fast-coming winter. She felt the land was not happy with the new conditions.

After a few moments of staring ahead, shapes began to re-emerge, a suggestion of Aitor's bright jacket, the bend of his elbow, a feeling of his face near hers. She almost had the sense of the driveway ahead of her, the walls on either side. It was acoustic as much as anything, a feeling of an area slightly better protected from the otherwise unchallenged wind.

'I feel like a bloody bat,' she murmured, as they began to walk carefully forwards down the drive.

As they moved Alice grew more confident and they gradually increased their speed to a near-normal walking pace. The drive had a few gravel-filled holes but was stable enough beneath their feet. After a gentle veer to the right, which Alice warned Aitor about when her foot struck a thick tuft of grass, they spotted a dim light ahead that signalled the farmhouse, or possibly one of the outhouses.

Instinctively they held hands as they moved forwards, finding it helped keep their footing steady. The light disappeared, blocked by trees or another building, and then became clear again. It was the front of the farmhouse, now they could see the rectangular window of what was most likely a living room. The wind grew, swelled, whistling through the stones of the wall on their right. They were pelted by a bout of freezing rain that Alice thought was going to properly drench them, but within a few paces it slowed and then stopped altogether.

Alice felt Aitor release her hand, watched as he took out the brightness of his phone.

'No signal here,' he said.

She checked hers. 'Same,' she said. 'But let's keep going.'

The drive came to an end and they moved behind the nearest of two vehicles in the courtyard, a minibus. They walked along the side and peered over the bonnet at the house, still some ten or more metres away. To their left, another light shone from a small window near the door, but everything else was in darkness.

'Do you think we can get a look in there?' said Alice, crouching down.

Aitor's eyebrows raised. 'They'll see us,' he said.

Alice chewed her lip. 'We could crouch along the wall and get below it. See if we can hear anything.'

'I'd be surprised,' said Aitor.

Alice looked at the house again. 'It's not double glazed,' she said. 'I think there's a chance.'

'Alice…'

'You're more scared of people than you are of ghosts,' said Alice, chuckling.

'You said it!'

'Come on.'

She darted to the rear of the Land Rover, parked in front of the minibus, closer to the house. Then, with the room light still far to the left of her, she crouched over and hurried towards the front of the house, certain she would be out of the sightline of anyone who wasn't right up against the window.

And froze, as a powerful security lamp flicked the whole courtyard into brightness.

Whilst she couldn't see or hear anything, Alice sensed – or imagined – the sudden change of mood in that living room, an urgent thumping about, possibly a rush towards the front door. She stood there, absorbing the change, for how long – a split second – then realised she needed to move.

'Alice!' Aitor hissed from behind the car.

She half-turned towards him, then another thought stopped her and she spun back towards the house.

'Come back!' he said, more loudly.

But she rushed towards the front of the house, towards the darker, nearer side.

There was a harsh clack, the lifting of a metal latch, and then the door swung inward. A woman strode out – a tall woman with long dark hair and glasses in a quilted jacket, someone Alice hadn't seen before. The woman's head began to turn towards her as she scanned the courtyard – but stopped as a loud shout came from behind Alice.

'Hello!'

Alice looked around as Aitor appeared at the front of the Land Rover, his bleached hair white in the glare of the security lamp. Alice's gaze locked on the logo on the passenger door, a stylised map of a river basin, as her mind whirled. Then she decided what to do.

Unnoticed, she turned and scuttled to the corner of the farmhouse where she ducked out of sight.

'Who are you?' said the woman. Her voice had a rich Lancashire edge to it.

'Can you help me, I'm lost?' said Aitor. Alice, peeping round the corner and trying to control her breathing, could see him, still standing his ground. Not moving towards the house.

'What? What do you…' began the woman.

'I'm looking for… er, Tiss, the village…'

'On foot?' said the woman. 'At night?'

'No, my car is at the top of the drive.' Alice could hear the shakiness his voice. He had always been so assured... She could also hear someone muttering in the doorway behind the woman, a man, who suddenly spoke out loudly:

'You're not far, mate,' he said. 'As you come out the drive, head right. Then take the second right. You'll get there.'

'Fine. Thanks. Thanks,' said Aitor. She feared he would glance at her, but instead he turned and began to walk away back up the drive.

'Who the hell was that…?' she heard the woman say, her voice dropping in volume as she turned back inside the house.

'Hold on, mate!'

Alice recognised the Black Country accent of Archie Jones. She saw Aitor stop and turn.

'Don't I recognise you?'

Aitor shrugged. 'Why?'

Alice risked a peek again, saw that Archie and another man, the tall one with glasses and the Kings of Leon T-shirt, were moving across the courtyard towards the Basque. The woman came into sight too.

'Aren't you that guy who does the paranormal blog – Aitor, isn't it?'

Aitor smiled, nervously. 'No, not me.'

'I'd recognise that accent and the hair anywhere,' said Archie. 'From the videos…'

'Uh…'

Alice needed to act, could almost feel Aitor's brain whirring with anxiety and indecision. Again, she expected him to glance at her, to give away her position but, amazingly, he controlled himself.

She gasped at what he did next.

77.

Aitor turned and ran, as fast as he could, away down the drive.

'Shit!' said the woman. 'Get him back, Blake!'

The man burst into a surprisingly quick run too, following Aitor and disappearing into the darkness up the drive.

A few more people spilled out of the house alongside the tall woman. Besides Archie, now in a black tracksuit, there was the old woman, Jemima, and one of the Greek girls. Then Alice ducked back behind the wall, terrified she might be seen.

'Who did you say he was?' said the dark-haired woman.

'He's one of these paranormal investigators,' said Archie. 'One of the more renowned ones, at least online. I subscribe to his feed. Lives down south. Basingstoke or somewhere like that. Doesn't bode well for us, that he's up here now. Doesn't bode well at all…'

'What are we going to do?' said the Greek girl.

'This is a bloody nightmare,' said the woman. Alice could hear the tension, verging on anger, in her voice. 'Blake had better catch him,' she continued, then added firmly: 'This is no coincidence…'

'Let's speed up,' said Archie. 'Go and get Ben…'

78.

Alice shut her eyes tight and tried to control her hyperventilation.

Surely they would hear her, they were only a few feet away? The thought made her panic more, her belly spasming with terror.

They had Ben! She and Aitor were right. What were they going to do with him?

And what had happened to Aitor? She couldn't bear the thought of them catching him. What might they do? Why had he done that, stood out from cover and given himself away like that?

There was only one thing she could think of. He had done it to give her a chance.

She shoved her mouth into the crook of her elbow, smothering a gasp in the softness of her fleece. What should she do? Go after them, try to help Aitor, try to defuse the situation?

No chance. These people meant business. She wouldn't be surprised at anything they might do to achieve their warped goal. She thought of Douglas, dead in his bed. Might they have…?

Surely not. They were twisted, evil enough to steal a child – but murder? She didn't think so, and yet…

There was something far darker going on here than she had expected.

She felt sick, sick to the depths of her struggling little soul. She had to help Ben. Aitor would have to fend for himself, he was smart, she was sure he would evade them...

So what was she going to do?

Clearly, she needed to get the police, to call Detective Tutt. Or 999? They might... She couldn't finish the thought, fished in her pocket, brought out her phone. No signal.

She dropped it as she went to put it back in her pocket.

'Did you hear that?' said the woman with the Lancashire accent.

Alice choked, almost sobbed. She'd thought they'd all gone back inside – she had to run! She glanced around, her surroundings still lit faintly by the grey-white light of the security lamp in the courtyard.

There was a small area fenced with chicken wire directly in front of her, a garden or vegetable patch by the looks of it, she could see a couple of spades or forks propped up against the gate. To her left, partially sheltered from the farmhouse by an arc of bamboo, was a raised single storey prefab with a long wooden porch. Without thinking, she ran over to it and hurled herself down on to the ground, then pulled herself under the porch into dark, damp weeds.

79.

She could see his boots, big black things, steel toe-capped working boots.

The man had a light source, probably the torch of his phone. He was swinging it about as he peered into the fenced vegetable patch, then he turned and strode towards the prefab, towards Alice, cheek pressed down into wet earth, holding her breath as her guts churned.

A boot came up, a few inches from her face, and thumped on to the wooden step in front of her eyes.

On the porch, the man paused, shining his light around. Alice blinked against its incandescence, in between the tiny gap in the porch floorboards. If he'd been looking down, she was sure he would have seen her eye staring up at him. But then he moved on, opening the door to the prefab, going inside. She heard his footsteps, crumping about the suspended floor. She closed her eyes but felt herself still looking up inside her head, to a point in between her eyebrows, a point of focus, of temporary transcendence. Or oblivion. She needed to get out of herself, for a moment, to get beyond her fear.

The man came out, thumped quickly down the stairs, and headed around the back of the building.

80.

Before doing anything, she checked her phone again.

Absolutely zero signal. Zilch. Nada.

What was she going to do?

Who were these people that had got her so damned… petrified?

Association. She thought about what had happened to her before, at Bramley manor. That was part of it, of this response, for sure. But how could she harness that experience to strengthen herself now?

She had to find Ben, before they did whatever they planned to do. She hoped she and Aitor were right, that they wanted to use his special ability to speak to the dead, that their intention wasn't something else entirely.

She tried to reassure herself about Aitor. He was one of the most resourceful men she'd ever met. She wouldn't put it past him to get back to his car before he was caught. And if that happened, if he made the right choices on weak information and specifically, if he made the right choice not to speak to them, not to try and come back for her – he could drive away to a place where he could get a signal.

Call the police.

It was her best hope. But even if he managed that… how long would it take them to get here?

All conjecture. She had no idea what would happen out there. For all she knew, the big man could have caught him, knocked him down with a single blow of his giant fist, and…

Stop.

She was on her own. She had to find Ben. She couldn't let what happened to her once, long ago, happen to him. A ten-year-old boy.

She would rescue him.

She swallowed. Even thinking big, dramatic things like that made her want to throw up.

81

Alice edged her way out from under the prefab.

She stood up and brushed herself down. She was wet and dirty from the water still sitting on the ground from the storm.

The dark was deeper now, the security lamp long since gone off, no lights on this side of the farmhouse. There was still a little light in front of her in the forecourt, probably from the living room. But she headed away from that into the deeper gloom at the rear of the house.

Her ankle bent sharply as she trod on an unseen object and she winced.

As she moved away from the prefab towards the rear of the farmhouse, she wished she could switch on her torch. She slipped on something else on the ground, a stone, but knew she couldn't risk the light.

Where were they likely to be holding Ben? Surely it would be better for her to leave the farm, try and get a signal, call the police. But… what if time was of the essence? She could never forgive herself if something dreadful happened that she could – just possibly – have prevented.

She came up to the edge of the house, peered in cautiously through a small, dark window, almost certainly not a major room, a toilet or utility room perhaps, or maybe just the end of a corridor. Inside, she could see very little so, after a quick glance left and right, flicked on her torch.

A tiled interior, the faint sheen of a long curtain, a shower unit fixed to the wall. It was a wet room, empty.

She turned off her light, walked to the next window. She was now close to the back of the house and her best guess was this would be the kitchen. As she was about to reach it, a fierce light flashed from the window, flashed again, and then remained, lighting up the gravel in front of her.

Alice pushed herself into the wall.

There was banging inside, voices she could hear through the original, single glazed sash windows. Mumbled voices, not a single word clear.

Could she move around the perimeter of the light so she could see inside, she wondered? She realised she would have to move out a long way, but there were some pine trees nearby she could use as cover. Now the light was on, she could also make out the barn beyond the trees, the one she and Ben had seen from the moors. She could see a small window in one corner of it, facing the house.

If she could get there, she would get a pretty good – and safe – view into the back of the house. And, who knew, perhaps there would be a signal in the barn and she could call the police. She could only hope.

There was a stab of pain in her side, anxiety, as she thought again of Aitor.

Then she retreated a little and forked out to the right, into the fringe of the pines.

82.

The wind was up again, she could hear it shushing through the pines as she made her way around the back of the farm. In between straight black trunks, she caught

167

the occasional glimpse of the kitchen light, of the movement of people inside – but the view wasn't clear enough to see who. She needed to get to that window in the barn…

Her eyes were becoming more accustomed to the night and she could vaguely make out the tall trunks ahead, sense their piney coats surging in the breeze in the dark. But still she managed to walk clumsily into a tree right in front of her, banging her shoulder hard. She cursed under her breath.

Soon she was through the small stand of trees and could see the dark imprint of the barn ahead of her. She crossed a messy patch of land strewn with tyres, sagging bags of compost or fertiliser, and a few pieces of unidentifiable farm machinery, then reached the edge of the building. She peered around the corner and into the first of the two huge, open doorways.

All dark. Not a hope of seeing a thing.

She pointed her torch at her feet, switched it on, and went in.

83.

Inside, she could feel the wind buffeting around, hear it jostling a large tarpaulin that was covering something in the near corner.

Alice was relieved to see there weren't any stock in the barn, no chickens or pigs to kick up a racket and give her away. Instead, it seemed to be used as an oversized tool shed, with long benches cluttered with the wood and metal bric-a-brac of construction and maintenance, hammers, chisels, files. The larger tools – billhooks, bowsaws, sledgehammers, axes, loppers, scythes, forks, slashers – hung from the walls, supported by screwed in straps.

Like the setting of a horror movie, Alice thought grimly.

She headed to the window at the rear. A bang made her spin round, her heart erupting against her ribcage – but it was only one of the giant, permanently tied-back doors knocking against the wall in the wind.

As she reached the window she heard something outside, a voice carried by the wind. Possibly even a shout, from the direction of the farm.

Followed by a crunching sound outside the giant shed. Without time to turn off her phone's torch, she jammed it in her pocket and ducked down behind the flapping tarpaulin.

Someone came into the barn. She heard him – she could be wrong, but from a small cough and the scuffing of footsteps it sounded like a man – move over to the bench. There were a few knocks and then moments later a scraping sound, like a heavy blade or screwdriver drawn down brick. Then the footsteps receded across the concrete floor and headed away down the far side of the building.

Alice, still doing her best to contain her erratic breathing, stayed still behind the tarpaulin.

There were more shouts outside, someone appeared to be coming closer to the barn again.

'Yeah, yeah, I'm coming,' a man called back. Possibly the big man with glasses, the one who had been chasing Aitor. What had happened to her friend…?

'Just getting a couple of things from the barn,' he said.

'We need to go now,' she heard the other person say, clearly closer now. 'They didn't…' and the voice was erased by the wind.

Alice waited, looking out of the giant doors at the black ink that concealed the moors. The wind whipped the canvas, flicking the hair at the side of her face.

She heard a distant engine start up, rumbling, loose, something in between a car and a tractor – the Land Rover.

A door banged, then another. Where were they going? Tiss?

But then the noise of the engine began to grow louder, groaning through the low gears and Alice realised…

The car was coming towards the barn.

84.

She watched as the track beside the barn lit up in the darkness, grainy at first then harsh and yellowish as the headlights got closer. The engine noise grew to an intense, pressurised growl.

Then the vehicle swerved in front of the barn and Alice risked a peek above the tarpaulin.

The Land Rover had two benches in the back that faced each other. Each was full of people, alongside two or three others on the long front seat. Alice couldn't recognise them in the poor light, it was just a group of silhouettes.

But one thing she could see, a thing that made her gasp and clutch hold of the tarpaulin – the figure in the

middle at the back was a good head shorter than the two
seated on either side of them.

'Ben…' she muttered.

85.

She stood up and ran over to the barn entrance.

She watched the taillights of the Land Rover as it
passed through a gateway in the drystone wall that
surrounded the farm. The headlights jerked about as the
vehicle began to lumber up the hillside, switching to
four-wheel drive for the pitted track.

What could she do? Head back down the drive and
see if she could find Aitor? Not very hopeful. Break into
the house and try and find a phone? Possibly. She had to
call the police, that much was sure. But what if there were
more people inside? And would the police be in time to
follow them… where? Where were they going?

Jackson's Rocks. Jackson's Rocks for their horrific
ritual to bring Ben into contact with the Devil of Tiss.
She was sure of it.

Her imagination threw up ghastly images of Horace
Clay and what he had done up there. She had to follow
them! She was the only one who knew what was
happening, who might have time to act. But what could
she do?

Her head felt like it was going to implode.

And then she had an idea.

86

She hurried back down to the farm, increasingly convinced now there was no one left to see her. They were all in this, who would want to miss this once in a lifetime opportunity?

A few of the windows of the farmhouse remained lit. As she approached the kitchen with its blue-green wall units she slowed and craned her neck to check as much of the interior as she could, just to be sure.

Empty. There was no one in there, assuming they weren't concealed in one of the narrow areas hidden from sight. There was a back door to the right of the window.

'Might as well…' she muttered and went up to it. It opened easily, thankfully, with just a slight squeak as the handle turned.

Alice stepped inside and found herself in a narrow corridor, with an opening into the kitchen beside her. The door had long since been removed, she noticed the splintered, chiselled out sections for the hinges. She peered into the kitchen, saw the mess of an uncleared communal supper, a large pot smeared with red sauce, stacks of unwashed plates and cutlery, glasses and plastic cups on a table stained with blotches of sauce. More saucepans and ceramic bowls were in the sink. They had clearly left in a hurry.

Alice didn't stop to look around. She was hoping to find two things. She hurried down the corridor, quickly checking two rooms with open doors before she passed them. One was a toilet – she screwed her nose up at the faint whiff of urine – and the other an office lit by a fluorescent strip, with shelves filled with box files, a desk and… a telephone. She stepped in, pushed the door closed behind her, and went over to the desk. There were a few printed papers scattered around a computer screen and keyboard. The hard drive hummed beneath the desk, tight up against the drawers. Alice snatched the phone from its cradle and held it to her ear.

No tone, no sound at all. She jabbed the switchhook. Nothing.

It was as if it was…

She reached over to the back of the desk and tugged at the cable. It was attached to the phone point. Hurriedly, she turned the phone round and pulled open the battery case.

Empty.

She pulled open a couple of drawers, sifted through stationery, business cards, other office bric-a-brac – but no batteries.

Why did they have a phone that didn't work. Or… had they removed them?

Maybe they were worried there might be someone else around, after Aitor's appearance. Maybe they weren't prepared to take any more chances.

She shuddered as she realised how much this set up must mean to them.

87.

Alice looked around the cluttered room, saw on the wall near the door a fire notice and a set of hooks with different keys. She went over and studied them, but they were all Yales, padlock or mortice keys, presumably for rooms and storage units around the farm. Not what she needed.

She went back out into the corridor and soon came into the front hall. A flight of carpeted stairs led up, opposite the front door, and there were rooms on either side. To the right was the living room, the light was still on and there was a battered linen sofa beneath the front window. The edge of a TV unit was also visible.

She was sure now there was no one left in the building. The house was still, the quiet almost palpable. Unless there was someone in a room upstairs, on the other side of the house, she was sure it was just her here. But still she needed to be quick.

As she hurried to the living room she spotted a small wooden tray on a table by the front door, in which were several more keys. She went closer and saw a ring with three door keys – and a black plastic vehicle key.

She snatched up the ring and, with a quick glance into the living room to check there was no one there, went to the front door and lifted the latch.

She ran out into the night, pushing the unlock button on the plastic key.

The lights of the van, still parked in the courtyard, flashed on and there was an electronic beep.

'Yes!' she cried.

And screamed, as a figure leapt out from behind the van.

88

'Alice!'

'Oh, thank God,' she cried, seeing Aitor approach. 'What happened?'

They grabbed hold of each other in a desperate hug.

'I realised the big guy was quicker than me,' said Aitor. 'So I ducked through a gate I'd noticed on the way in and hid for a while until he gave up and came back. I was going to come straight back to find you but realised I had a signal…'

'Fantastic!' said Alice, thinking how his night vision was clearly better than hers.

'Only one bar, but yes, I got through to the police. 999.'

'They're coming?'

'Yes. I got cut off first time but moved a bit further away from the house and made a good call. I told them it was in relation to Ben, and we had reason to believe he might be held here. That they'd chased me off the premises – and that you might be in danger.'

'That's great, Aitor,' said Alice. 'But…'

'But what?'

'We need to go after them. They've all gone. And I think they've taken Ben with them.'

'Gone where?' said Aitor.

'After I'd hid for a while, I went round the back to a barn to try and get a good look in the house. But soon after the Land Rover came past, heading out the back on the track up the hill. They were all in it and… Aitor, they had Ben with them! I could tell from the size of him, he was sandwiched in between two adults. My guess is they were going to the Rocks. I'm certain of it, Aitor.'

'Shit.' Aitor sucked air through his teeth.

'We need to go after them,' said Alice. 'The police will be too late.'

'We could call the police from the farm landline. There must be a…'

'Forget it. They've taken the phone batteries out. They must have thought you might come back, didn't want to take the risk you might use it…'

Aitor bit his lip, then said: 'We can go back to where I got the signal – try and call the police again. Tell them where we think they're going.'

'How far was it?'

'A few minutes' walk – four or five.'

There was a decision to make. Alice felt a surge, a physical pressure, pushing at the back of her skull. A flicker of panic, a crushing sense of hopelessness… She had to hold it back, she remembered the fire in Farthingbridge, the split-second choices she'd had to make then.

She nodded. 'Get in the van,' she said, opening the driver door. 'We'll go up the drive, try and get the signal again.'

Aitor nodded and pulled open the passenger door.

89.

The vehicle was a clunky thing, but luckily Alice had driven a few vans and minibuses in her time and she handled it well on the pitted drive. As she drove, Aitor repeat dialled 999, hoping for the signal to connect.

She braked hard at the end of the drive as Aitor said: 'Hello… Yes, police, please…'

'Thank God,' she said.

'Hello… hello… Shit! It's cut out.'

Alice looked left and right, down the country lane. She could make out a few trees on either side, rocking in the wind, before the road disappeared into disheartening blackness.

'One more time,' Aitor said quietly, his face a pale, bluish glow beside her, his finger jabbing at the screen.

Alice switched into gear and spun the van round in a tight circle to be facing back down the drive towards the farm.

'What are you doing?' he said. 'I've got a bar…'

She stopped the van sharply. 'One more try,' she said. 'If that doesn't work, we're going on our own.'

'But it might be stronger down the…' Aitor looked at her. 'Your mind is made up, isn't it?' he said.

90.

As the van rocked back up the drive towards Bracken Hill Farm, Aitor snapped open the glove compartment. He pulled out the vehicle manual, fished around amongst odd scraps of paper, reached right to the back and found what he was looking for.

'Ouch!' he cried, as the van dipped in a pothole and he bashed his head on the dashboard.

'Sorry,' said Alice.

'It's OK,' he said, sitting back and rubbing his forehead. He reached up and switched on the overhead light, then turned a printed sheet of paper over on its blank side and placed it on the manual. He pulled the top of the biro he'd found off with his teeth and began scribbling on the sheet.

When they reached the courtyard, Alice swung the vehicle round sharply and stopped by the front door. Aitor leapt out and dashed to the door. She watched him in the glare of the security lamp as he looked around, thinking, then lifted the flap of the letter box and let it trap the top edge of the paper. Even in the poor light, she could read the giant capitals he had printed on it, in his narrow handwriting that reminded her of stick men:

MESSAGE TO THE POLICE

MISSING BOY BEN DAVIS
IS AT JACKSON'S ROCKS - POSSIBLY CLAY
CAVE OR AMPHITHEATRE -
IN THE HANDS OF KIDNAPPERS
IMMEDIATE ASSISTANCE REQUIRED

7.15PM SUNDAY

Moments later he slammed back into the seat beside her.

'Come on. Let's go!'

91.

It was a good, solid van, but with the ordinary road tyres and absence of four-wheel drive the going was tough. Very tough.

Alice maintained a fierce concentration, keeping up the revs to prevent slipping or stalling, fighting to maintain the track within the headlights. The trail was soaked in places, steep in others, deeply gouged in more – but better by far than having to navigate through the clumpy grass and heather that made up the rest of the moorland. Without this dirt track they would have grounded ages ago or worse still, rolled.

She heard Aitor grunt as they lurched into another hole. She stayed on the throttle and prayed they wouldn't tip.

'We won't make it the whole way,' she said, gritting her teeth as a loud bang came from beneath and the vehicle shook.

'Just as far as we can,' said Aitor. 'It'll save us time, no matter what. We wouldn't want to… shit!'

They cried out as the van tipped precariously down the slope, both instinctively leaning to try and stop the thing from overbalancing. Alice steered down into the possible roll, then swung the wheel back as soon as she'd regained some control. The van swerved, bounced, then steadied on the track.

'Good driving,' said Aitor. 'I thought we were goners then.'

Overhead, at the top of the windscreen, Alice saw the grey cloud cover breaking, revealing a misty moon.

'What were you saying?' she said.

'What?' he said. 'Oh yes. We don't want to go the whole way, anyway. At some stage – depending on where they are on the Rocks, and what they're doing – they might hear us, or see the headlights. We're better off stopping a little distance away and walking the final stretch.'

'Good thinking,' said Alice, trying to remember the lay of the land from the couple of times she had walked to the Rocks. 'There's a gentle ridge we come to soon,' she said. 'Jackson's Rocks is a couple of hundred metres on from it. If we stop before that, we should be well out of sight – and earshot, given the wind.'

'Sounds good.'

Alice wrestled with the wheel as the van slithered around on a wet patch. A few stunted thorns showed at the side of the makeshift track in the erratic beam of the lights. Above them, Alice noticed the moon had once again vanished, smothered by deep cloud. The back end of the van began to slip outwards. She reduced the revs but it continued to rotate sideways before stalling and sliding to a halt.

'How far to that ridge?' said Aitor, as she pushed the ignition button and the engine kicked back into life.

'Not far,' she said. 'This little beauty's done a lot better than I expected up here.'

They were silent for a while as Alice switched to sidelights and dropped the revs. She felt the tension in her shoulders and there was a pain starting at the back of her neck, a stress headache. In some ways the driving was good, though, it took her mind off…

'Alice?'

'Mm.'

'What are we going to do when we get there?'

'I haven't got a clue,' she said, shaking her head.

Summoning the Devil

92.

'Well done,' said Alice.

'Are you talking to yourself or the van?' said Aitor, as they came to a halt.

'The van. It's a miracle. I thought we'd get halfway but now… here we are.'

'It's your driving, darling,' said Aitor. 'It's fantastic.'

They climbed out, shutting their doors carefully, and began to walk along the track. After a moment Aitor slipped and Alice reached out and took his hand.

Their eyes grew accustomed to the dark, aided by an occasional pearliness in the sky, the moon attempting to make another appearance. The path began to slope heavily and this time it was Alice's turn to slip. Her knee went down into wet mud and Aitor had to help her up again.

'This must be the ridge,' she said. Moments later, as the path levelled, she knew she was right.

'Look, there!' said Aitor.

The blackness ahead of them was no longer complete. In the distance was a faint pinprick of yellow, like a candlelight.

'It's on the Rocks, I reckon,' said Alice. 'Come on…'

As they drew nearer it became clear what the light was. A fire.

'I think it's in the amphitheatre,' said Alice. 'It looks about the right height, up near the top.'

'OK,' said Aitor.

'We need a plan,' said Alice.

'Yes,' said Aitor.

They carried on in silence.

93.

Soon they could see the glow of the fire more clearly, high on the rocks looming above them.

Alice recognised the patch of woodland where she had encountered the group clearing vegetation. Before it, they found the Land Rover parked at a tilt.

They hurried up to the vehicle and used Aitor's phone torch to peer inside. When they saw it was empty, they carried on into the woods.

The trees crowded in on them and the space became once again perilously dark. Alice took out her phone, checking again for a signal before she switched on the torch and shone it at their feet.

'Keep it down,' said Aitor.

They picked their way over smaller stones, in between clumps of scrub, Alice leading the way. Soon they found the path that led up the Rock. They climbed quickly and reached the elevated point above the moor. The moon broke out and they had a view of the great sweep of fuzzy, spidery grass stretching out below them, down into the valley.

'Amazing,' Aitor muttered.

'At least I can switch off my light,' said Alice. The limestone gave an almost phosphorescent glow in the moonlight, although it quickly faded as they headed back into an area overgrown with trees and shrubs. Nevertheless, there was just enough light for them to make their way. And soon, up above, they could see the glow of the firelight in the night sky.

'Must be the amphitheatre,' said Alice.

'Shh,' said Aitor. 'Can you hear?'

Alice stopped. The wind had dropped to a steady breeze. She could hear – faintly – the sound of someone speaking. A monologue, perhaps a reading. She shivered, remembering Bramley, and felt Aitor's arm around her shoulder.

'You're alright,' he said, quietly.

'I know,' she said. 'Thank you.'

'We're going to have to be careful from now on,' he said.

'At least I know the ground,' said Alice. 'Keep near.'

'Yes. When we get there… we'll see what they're doing. Then figure out what to do.'

'Are we mad, Aitor?' she said. 'Shouldn't we wait for the police?'

'We can always do that,' he replied. 'We don't have to intervene. If there's no immediate danger to Ben – well, we can sit it out and wait for them to get here.'

'If they got our notice,' said Alice. 'And if they decide to act on it.'

'They will. What choice do they have?'

She could hear the uncertainty in his voice. The police would certainly come. If they found the note. If it hadn't been blown away by the wind.

But – assuming they did find it – might it be too late?

94

The wind buffeted, rattling the dried leaves that remained on the trees, as they climbed the rough-hewn steps to the amphitheatre.

Then, as they were nearing the top, it dropped again. Looking up, Alice could see the light spilling from the ledge above them. And, as they stood still, they could hear. Hear them speaking.

'Relight it, Leanda,' said a woman's voice, one of the Greeks, Alice was sure. She scrambled around an outcrop of rock, levering herself up into a small cranny where she could peek out. Behind her, Aitor squeezed in too.

'What the…?' he whispered.

Alice shook her head in disbelief. In the performance area of the amphitheatre, there were two figures visible – Stella and Leanda. The fire pits had been lit and whilst the one at the far end was still blazing, the nearest had been extinguished, presumably by the wind. One of the women, dressed in a red robe, was attempting to relight it, a few metres away from Alice. In the dimness, Alice was just able to make out that she held a small plastic petrol can. Behind her, in the middle of the theatre, the other woman was similarly dressed. She was down on her hands and knees, drawing a shape on the bare rock with a piece of chalk.

'Where are the others?' said Aitor.

'I don't know, but I've had enough of this,' said Alice, feeling a sudden anger. She stood up and clambered over the boulder.

The nearby woman, whom the other had called Leanda, straightened as she saw Alice approaching. Casually, she flicked something from her waist on to the fire, a flaring match. An orangey flame whooshed up from the pit.

'Who's this then…?' she said in her heavily accented voice.

'You know who I am,' said Alice, striding towards her. 'Where's the boy?'

'Who?'

'The boy! Ben. What have you done with him?'

In the brightness of the fire, the girl's dark eyes blazed. She seemed to be smirking. Alice could hear Aitor scrambling over the rocks behind her.

'Stella,' said the woman, without looking back at her cousin.

The other stopped drawing – it was another pentagram, Alice could see now, like the one in the cellar – and started walking towards them.

'You're the Spanish one, aren't you?' said Stella, looking over Alice's shoulder at Aitor. Her hair was longer than her cousin's, but loose, tied at the back in a ponytail.

Aitor snorted. With a swift movement, Stella pulled one side of the robe away, revealing her naked body in the firelight.

Alice stepped around the firepit and grabbed Leanda's arm.

'Where are they?'

She felt the woman relax in her grip, become pliant. She was slightly taller than Alice and looked down at her softly. She said something Alice couldn't hear in the wind.

'What?' said Alice.

'Dig…' again the words were lost in the wind.

Alice, feeling increasingly volatile, shook her arm and stood close to her, almost nose to nose.

'Again!' she said.

'Dig deep and release your core,' said Leanda, and smiled at her. 'Your demonic core…'

Alice slapped her cheek. Hard.

Leanda gripped her jaw, then released it. She smiled again. 'Yes,' she said. 'Bring it out, you have a talent for it.'

Stella was approaching Aitor, sashaying her hips in an exaggerated fashion. 'Come on, Spanish boy,' she said. 'Dance with me.'

'Who are these people?' said Aitor.

'They're not going to tell us anything,' said Alice. 'I think they realised they might be followed. They're a distraction. Come on!' She turned and grabbed him by the wrist. 'Let's go.'

'Stay with us,' said Leanda to Alice. 'Tonight's the night and you have a lot to give. I can sense it.'

Alice ignored her and turned to run across the amphitheatre, holding Aitor's arm. Stella flashed her body at him again as they ran past, her breasts white in the cold, the dark hair between her crossed legs. Aitor glared at her, incredulous.

Then, suddenly, she grabbed his wrist and pulled him back. He pushed out his elbow and she stumbled back, then tripped and hit the ground. She remained on her back, still, her eyes closed.

'Shit…' said Aitor. He was interrupted by a shriek, spun to see the other woman, Leanda, running towards him.

Alice stepped forward and struck her on the side of the face with her fist. The woman spun round, joy dancing in her eyes.

'You liked that didn't…' she began.

Alice swung her fist up and hit her under the jaw. Leanda crashed down by her cousin.

'We need to…' said Aitor, starting to kneel by the women.

'No – they'll be alright,' said Alice, shaking her hand, which hurt like hell. She could see Stella groaning, her eyes fluttering open and closed. She wondered if they might be drugged up, they both went down so easily. 'Come on, we have to find the others!'

Aitor glanced back at the women uncertainly, and then submitted to the tug of Alice on his sleeve.

They were off, running along the path that circumnavigated the great Rock.

95.

'They *were* a decoy…'

'You sure?' said Aitor, as they slowed and began to pick their way around the darker side of the rock, using the torches again. 'I hope they're OK…'

'They will be,' said Alice. 'They really don't want this thing, whatever it is they're doing, to get interrupted. They've clearly put a lot of time and effort into planning it.'

'And now the police are involved they're panicking…' said Aitor.

'Yep.'

'So where next – the cave?'

'Yep.'

There was a low cooing sound from the drop to their right, an owl declaring its territory, alerting Alice to the fact the wind had stopped again. She could feel something inside her, something immense and frightening. It made her realise that walking out here, in the night, on this unsteady path, was quite helpful. It helped keep her mind off it.

Off her anger. Her vast, all-consuming fury.

96.

'They're in there,' said Aitor.

There was light spilling from the plinthed entrance to the cave. Light and, as they paused and listened, an echoey, human sound…

Singing. No – chanting.

'What are they up to?' said Alice, starting to speed towards the portal.

She was stopped by Aitor's grip on her arm.

'Wait.'

She looked at him in the torchlight.

'These people are dangerous, Alice,' he said.

She knew he was right. Hadn't she seen it before?

'What are we going to do?'

'Alice – what are we prepared to do?'

Oh God. That question. Why did he have to ask it, to highlight it? So stark…

'I can, I will…' she said. 'I will hurt them. If they are hurting him. I'll… kill them!'

She knew it was true. She had a capacity inside her, an aggression, a willingness to inflict physical harm – only for those things she cared about, justice, love, innocence, surely? – something she rarely experienced, but now…

Something she had felt at Peacehaven but later put down to circumstance. But something she now knew was true. Even if it wasn't right.

'OK,' said Aitor, sucking in his breath. 'Let's do this. We'll go in together.'

The clarity of violence – of anticipated, imagined violence – drained Alice's fury, even though she had been ready for it moments ago. She felt a giddiness, the snuffing of her will.

'Aitor, we could be wrong about it all. There's more of them than us…'

She noticed something about him had changed. He was more upright, fired up, more… alert.

Then she heard it.

The sound of a boy shrieking.

Without a thought, Alice ran into the cave.

97.

The floor of the inner chamber had a new pentagram, which must have been swiftly drawn in chalk by the acolytes.

Two large candelabra, each with a dozen or more candles, lit the area, symmetrically placed at the centre of the pentagram where the occultists were gathered, each in a red robe like the two in the amphitheatre.

Alice saw a man with bushy hair and a moustache, someone she'd not seen before, standing towards the edge, clutching a long-handled slasher; the bow-backed lady, Jemima, now wearing garish eyeliner and red lipstick, with her husband, Charles, both pressing their hands together as if in prayer; and, in the middle, on either side of Ben, Archibald Jones and the woman with glasses and dark hair who had appeared at the door of the farm. Archie was reading from a book that looked too big to hold in one hand. The woman held a broad-bladed dagger up against the boy's chest.

All this Alice took in before meeting Ben's bewildered glance, seeing the beg in his eyes.

'Stop this!' she shouted.

The woman with the dark hair threw back her head and laughed.

'What?' said Alice.

'We've stepped on to a bloody film set,' Aitor muttered.

'Nice to see you again, Alice,' said Archie. 'I had an inkling you might turn up, didn't I, Mel?'

'What do you mean?' said Alice.

'Get the knife away from the boy!' shouted Aitor, beside her.

Melissa looked at them and said: 'Blake!'

Alice glanced to her side, saw no one there, turned to look the other way…

And heard Aitor cry, raising his hands, staggering in front of her. She saw the tall man Blake barging into him, towering over him, striking down at him with his arm, no, with an axe, he had an…

She saw dark liquid flying around in the air, heard a tortuous noise, stumbled back as somebody hit and bounced away from her. Glanced down to see the Basque with his eyes closed tight in pain, clasping his neck, on the ground.

Looked up to see the giant man, ruthlessly, mercilessly, stepping towards her, his arm bending at the elbow in a neat, contained motion, bringing up the short-hafted axe, ready to strike her…

98.

'Stop!'

It was a child's voice, a boy's shriek.

Everyone stopped, including Blake, the axe inches away from the middle of Alice's brow. All eyes turned to Ben.

Held by Archie and Melissa, the boy was pointing off to the right.

'He's come!' he said.

They all looked where he was pointing.

And Alice saw him, with his leather suit and ram's horns, with his leather tail and bear claw gloves.

The Reverend Horace Clay.

The Devil of Tiss.

Wearing his torn, swollen, woman's face.

99.

In a swift blur, the ghost moved in from the edge of the pentagram.

This time, Alice didn't feel the same terror. At least, not for the foul spirit, not now she knew who he was, just a man. But she was scared for Aitor and scared for the boy. Just no longer for herself, despite the hatchet inches away from her head.

'What's he say?'

It was Melissa, head askance, speaking to the boy.

Alice could see the eagerness, desperation, awe on her face – on all the faces of the cult, turned towards the red ghost. Although, as she watched the woman, she realised she wasn't looking at the ghost, but rather at a point a little to its side. Glancing around, Alice saw the same was true of all the group. They were looking broadly in the right direction but, because none of them had the ability to see ghosts, they were glancing about anxiously. She heard Charles whisper to Jemima: 'Where is he? Can you see him, dear?'

'Yes, I think…' said Jemima, but she was looking a good few feet to the side of the ghost.

Alice watched as Ben stepped forward with a scowl, towards Horace Clay. Time seemed to drain away again, like when she'd encountered the Devil in the cellar, suspended in morbid fascination, in the grip of the grotesque, of things outside the natural order.

Ben raised his head, frowned, sneered, wiped his eyes with his forearm.

'What do you want?' he said, sullenly.

The spirit, its thick, leather tail seemingly dragging across the floor, drew up to him. Alice could see the boy looking up, struggling to maintain eye contact with those evil, beady eyes, set deep in the mess of another's flesh.

'I know,' said Ben. 'Yes, I know. You realised what I could do when you heard us talking, so what? … Yes… what do you want?'

Whilst everyone was quiet, watching the boy staring up at the nothing that they saw, Alice dropped to her knees, not caring if her movement made Blake strike. She looked at Aitor, saw that the frown had gone from his face now, his eyes were closed, eyebrows raised, as if he was sleeping…

'No,' she whispered, easing his slackened hand away from the wound. Even here in the shadows, far from the candlelight, she could see the gash near his neck, the dark blood oozing out…

She pressed her hand on top of it, trying to staunch the flow. Above her, the giant man continued to gaze at the spectacle in the pentagram. She looked over again.

Ben's eyes opened wide as the apparition surged back and forth at him, spewing its bilious message. A child should never know the mind of a man like that, she thought. *Hopelessly.*

Eventually, the ghost paused, drew back a little, and waited.

Ben turned and looked up at the two adults, Melissa and Archie.

'Come on,' said Melissa, placing the knife against the side of his neck. 'What's he say?'

'There's no need to do that,' said Ben. 'I'm not fighting.' He took a breath and said: 'He says he wants a body.'

'Yes, course he does, the Reverend Clay wants to live, doesn't he? Obvious,' said Archie. He stared at a point that might have been the ghost's head. 'Who doesn't, eh? We're going to have to find you someone to…'

'And there's more,' said Ben. 'He says he wants…' he grimaced in the candlelight. 'He says he wants a face…'

'A face?' said Charles quietly, looking at Jemima, who was looking back at him with raised eyebrows.

'Yes,' said the moustachioed man. 'Like the one he took from Gretel. Perhaps it'll help him manifest?'

Melissa seized Ben's shoulder. 'Ask him!' she hissed. 'Ask him what it is like – on the other side!'

Ben held her gaze for a split second – pitilessly, thought Alice, crouching with her friend.

'OK,' he said. He turned back to Clay.

'You heard her,' he said. 'They want to know what it's like – only being half dead.'

100.

Alice felt the tension rise in the damp chamber, the sense of anticipation. All around, candlelight flickered on the serried crops of stone.

Ben frowned, sneered, watched the spirit stonily as it loomed above him. At times, it seemed to Alice its smoky edges were overlapping, soaking into the boy. She wondered at the boy's composure, the way he kept a steely calm in his eyes.

Eventually, the boy turned away and looked back round at the gawping acolytes.

'He says it's the moment of the greatest betrayal. The memory… of what again?' Ben paused, head cocked slightly to the side, then said: 'He says it's the memory of a lifetime's dark nudges. A place where you *cannot* dwell – but must. It's insufferable, it's not home, it's… Unhome. It's the opposite of home and he hates it. Loathes it. And he… he demands you get him out of there.'

'Demands…?' said Melissa, quietly.

She was interrupted by a sharp noise, repeating, coming from outside of the cave. A dog, thought Alice. It was a dog barking.

'What the hell…?' said Melissa.

The barking grew louder. There was the sound of people shouting.

'Quick!' said Melissa and she jumped on Ben's back, forcing him to the ground on his face. The boy cried out sharply. 'If Clay can possess him we can find out more!'

Alice sprang up intending to run towards them, then dived sideways as Blake swung the axe at her. She felt it bump against her hip but she was away, almost stumbling over her own feet. The big man lunged after her as she charged towards Ben and Melissa.

'Take him, Clay, in him!' screamed Melissa, looking anxiously about at the roof of the cave.

Alice saw the ghost loom above them, emanating menace. Archie dropped to his knees and helped pin the boy down.

More shouts from outside, a higher pitched yapping. They were close.

Alice shrieked as the old man, Charles, tried to grab hold of her, faster, more dextrous than she ever would have imagined. He caught her right forearm tightly with both hands and she punched him, hard as she could, on the bridge of the nose with her other hand. He cried out, staggered back, clutching at a bloody streak.

She was free, running towards the three figures at the centre of the pentagram, seeing the Devil of Tiss seeming to twirl about above Ben's head, still pressed against the dirt floor by Archie's hands –

And then she was falling, tripped by something, someone, the woman, Jemima, and she hit the ground hard, painfully, managed to roll over on to her side, to look up and see the old woman with a look of violent glee on her face, raising her robed leg to stamp on her, and the big men, Blake and the one with the curly mullet, bearing down on her with blades, and Aitor motionless by the door and a riot of noise and still, regardless of the danger, she looked to Ben and the Devil and saw the boy struggling, shouting, the Reverend's ghost swelling then shrinking...

And then Alice looked back and, in the midst of all the din, the screaming and thumping and shouting, she saw Blake once again raising the hatchet to chop her and...

101.

'Police, drop it...!'

A bang, followed by a rapid clicking noise, like a scrambling arachnid on steroids.

Alice saw the big man fall and she rolled sideways, but still he managed to collapse across her lower body. She grunted with the shock and pain and then there was a crashing and clunking and out of the corner of her eye she saw the two candelabra crash to the ground and the lights went out.

For a moment it seemed as if the darkness was complete. There was shouting, grunting, screaming, and the frenzied barking of dogs. Something swept across Alice's face, a creature, she thought, a bat, and then realised she was completely mistaken, it was a light, a lightning sharp torch beam, presumably from the police.

She looked sideways, towards the centre of the pentagram, from where she was lying prostrate on the ground. Torch beams swirled about, strobing the cavern, but it remained mostly dark. She saw the ghostly figure of Horace Clay, lit by its own infernal light, hovering over a shape, Ben, still pinned by Archie. Melissa was still there too. Alice guessed it must have either been her – or possibly Archie, if he stretched – who had shoved over the candelabra to cast the room in near-darkness.

'No!' Alice cried, pointing in the dark. 'Over there! The boy's over there! Help him!'

But the torch beam arrived on her face and she was blinded. 'Over there!' she screamed, pointing from beneath Blake. She could feel her trousers were soaking and hoped she hadn't wet herself, then thought it might be the big man's blood. Had they shot him?

She glanced to the side again and couldn't see Archie or Ben, it was too dark – but she could see the Devil, Horace Clay, and he was changing, shrinking, swirling about like a dust devil, but closing down, going down into the ground… Or was he? Might he be…

'Stop, don't move, put your hands above your head now!'

She ceased struggling beneath the dead weight of the giant man. Looking up she could see the flashlight, her vision was wiped out, then lifting an arm to screen her eyes, she could see a bulky man in black above her, pointing something, *a pistol?,* at her face, shouting:

'Don't move! Don't move!'

'I'm not, I won't!' she shouted, lifting her arms.

There was more clumping about, shouting, wailing, Alice glimpsed light beams starting to fix on members of the cult, officers yelling at them to stop. Jemima was shrieking and kicking as a policewoman pinned her around the arms and chest.

Alice relaxed her neck and gazed up at the dark shape above her, staring at her along the smooth line of the gun barrel.

'Help the boy,' she said. 'And my friend in the corner, he's hurt.'

And she noticed the other dark figures who had stormed the room, grabbing and chucking people to the ground, shouting, commanding people to stop, freeze, stay where they were. A dog barked ferociously as it reared on its back legs, restrained by its leash.

And then, as she watched the motionless stance of the officer above her, everything became a daze.

102.

'Alice – Alice are you alright?'

She was sitting outside the cave on the path, back against the wall, covered in a thermal blanket. A woman in green and yellow was applying something to the side of her hip, a cream that stung. There were lots of people around, mainly police. Lots of talking, the distortion of voices on radios.

She looked up as the middle-aged man in a dark jacket sat down in front of her.

'I'm DI Tutt,' he said. He looked at the paramedic kneeling beside her, as if she wasn't there. 'Is she OK?'

The woman, blonde hair in a ponytail, nodded. 'Only a light cut here. Her knuckles are bruised. And she's in shock.'

'OK.' The Inspector stood up and turned away.

'Wait!'

He looked back.

'Inspector,' said Alice, remembering the pentagram, the last thing she saw there. 'We need to find Ben – where's Ben?'

'He's OK,' said the Inspector. 'We've taken him away.'

'Where? I need to see him!'

'To the station. There's a safe place for him there. He'll be alright.'

'No, but…' She realised the hopelessness of trying to explain why she needed to see him. 'I – he knows me, so…'

'I'll get you to him as soon as these guys,' he gave a smile to the paramedic, 'have given you the OK.'

Alice frowned, gripped by panic.

'He's OK,' the Inspector said again, trying to reassure her.

'Uh, and Aitor… my friend… how is he?'

'Aitor…'

'What?' Alice felt a sharp pain in her chest. 'What?' she said again.

'He's alive. His injury was serious. He's on his way to hospital.'

Alice glanced at the paramedic treating her, who tried a kindly smile. Alice blinked, looking quickly from left to right, not seeing anything.

The Visit

103.

Later, she was sitting in a waiting room in a police station somewhere in Sheffield.

The lighting from two overhead discs was warm, but the moss-green chairs with their blond wooden arms that matched the coffee table were somehow dispiriting. A yucca stood beside her, a little too close. The tips of its leaves kept tickling the top of her head as she shifted around in the seat. The two magazines on the table – *Good Housekeeping* and *Men's Health* – were a whole world away.

She wanted to be back home but knew she must wait. She had to see Ben – and give her statement.

The door opened and her heart lifted, only to see a police constable without the boy.

'Want another cup of tea?' the woman said. She was middle-aged, her grey hair in a neat bob.

'No – actually, yes,' she replied, and the woman disappeared.

Alice stood up and looked out of the window at a dark, rain-sodden street, at the hunched streetlights and a solitary black cab passing by.

104.

But when the officer opened the door next, Alice could hear her chuckling. She was followed into the room by Ben, clutching his Sheepy, and by another woman in jeans and sweatshirt.

As soon as he saw Alice, Ben ran up and threw his arms around her, trapping the sheep against her hip. Alice hugged him tight as the women watched.

'Are you OK?' she asked, pressing her cheek into his hair.

'Yes,' he said.

'How did they get you?' she said.

'Sheepy. They must have taken him that night,' he replied.

They released each other and stepped back. Alice looked him up and down.

'My grandad…' he said. His face crumpled.

'Yes…' said Alice and clutched him again as he sobbed. She felt his chest shudder and wanted to absorb all that pain into her, to physically take it in through her body. She wondered how much pain this room, neutral, beige, warm, had absorbed.

Alice looked across the top of the boy's head at the policewoman, whose face was strained with compassion. She saw the other woman, possibly a social worker, also watching with concern.

'Did they hurt you?' said Alice.

Once again they drew apart. She looked keenly at his face for any sign of bruising, for any sign of… something else.

'No,' he said.

'You were in that farmhouse all the time?' said Alice.

'Yes, they locked me in a room upstairs. But I was OK.'

'We've got them all now,' said the policewoman.

'Did you capture the two in the amphitheatre?' said Alice. 'The Greek women?'

'Yes,' said the woman. 'The Sarge says they got them all, all seven of them. Those two had made it all the way back to the farm, they were packing their bags to flee. They tried to run and there was a scuffle, our officers had to taser them, like they did with that chap who was going for you…'

Alice noticed a sudden embarrassment in the woman's eyes. She was probably not meant to share details like that, anything that could be construed as satisfaction with the use of force.

'Thank God,' she said. She held Ben's face, looked deeply into his eyes. How could she tell…?

'Don't,' he said.

'What?'

'Keep looking at me like that…'

'Sorry.' Alice released him and turned to the constable. 'What happens… with Ben now?'

'We've got an Emergency Protection Order in process with Children's Services,' she said. 'It's a formality of course, as there's no other family…' She winced slightly as the boy stared at her disbelievingly.

'We have some lovely people who will look after you,' said the other woman with a kind smile. 'I'll be making sure you get the very best…'

Alice saw Ben grimace and tighten his grip on Sheepy's neck.

'You'll be alright,' she said. She reached out to touch him but he flinched away.

'How do you know?' he said. 'It could be anyone.'

Alice nodded. How was he ever going to trust people again?

And… how could she be sure what she'd seen in those final moments in the cave wasn't that despicable spirit pouring its foul essence into the child, taking possession of him?

She had learnt first-hand the cunning a ghost could exhibit when they finally took hold of someone.

How could she be sure Horace Clay wasn't intertwined in Ben Davis right now, deadly but hidden, like a snake in the grass?

105.

When Ben had gone, another police officer showed up, a friendly but hesitant Sergeant by the name of Clive Devon. He took a statement from Alice and then, after she had rejected his suggestion of staying in the city at a local guest house, he arranged for yet another pair of officers to drive her home.

106.

And now here she was, back at Victor's cottage. Alone.

Alone in the dull, early morning light, sprawling on the couch, staring out the window and thinking, how would she ever sleep?

Alice thought about coffee, cereal, toast… no. Nothing. She couldn't eat or drink. How was Ben? Who was he with now? It could be anyone, surely a couple, almost certainly a foster family in the city – or was he still in the care of the police or the council? How would he cope, used to a quiet, introverted life in the country with just his grandad?

And Aitor, that terrible wound to his shoulder, so close to his neck, how was he now, right now? Alive, thankfully, Inspector Tutt had called and told her he had had an operation and a blood transfusion, and his condition was now critical but stable…

Those people…

How could they do this, use people, kidnap a child, all to what end? To discover the truth about death? Where had it all lead? Just to some cryptic, dispiriting remarks that could mean anything. She needed Aitor back, to talk to him, to feel safe with him, the only person in the world who she knew she could trust…

There was so much bombarding her mind, it felt like a physical pulse, a carpet bombing of her brain. And, in the middle of it all, there was something fleeting, significant, something important from the last few hours she needed to bring up whole and crisp into her conscious mind, she knew…

But what?

What was it she needed to remember?

God, she needed to…

Have a moment of oblivion.

107

Someone was repairing the house.

Victor, her boss, he'd told her there was a problem with the roof, some tiles missing or something. And now someone had arrived, they were hammering away.

Thump, thump, thump.

She should go up there, offer to make him a cup of tea, it was cold outside, probably still raining.

Thump, thump.

Oh, awake.

There was light, proper, grey light, fuzzy, through her lashes, she could see that ceramic bowl with the painted peacock and the satsumas…

Alice sat up.

She had been asleep. Her brain was weighed down at the front, like a sinking ship, going down, down into deep water. Had she been dreaming…?

There was another clunk, a second clunk. Somewhere outside the lounge, in the hall.

She'd been dreaming, there was no one doing the roof. Victor had talked to her about it, wanted her to keep an eye on the damp patch on the ceiling in the bathroom, in case it grew, but… he hadn't scheduled any repair work.

So what she was hearing was…

Thump, thump.

The door. Someone was banging on the front door.

She pushed herself up using the arm of the sofa – she was so groggy, like she'd been drinking – and moved out into the hall. Up to the door.

And stopped.

Who was it? It was – she looked into the kitchen – still daylight, of course, she'd seen that in the lounge, the natural light when she woke – God, she was disorientated…

But she could have been asleep for six hours or six minutes. No way of knowing. Who was at the door?

She wished she had a peep hole. Perhaps she should leave it. But what if it was the police, come to speak to her about Ben – or Aitor…

She took a deep breath, tried to summon her acuity. Reached forward and took hold of the latch. Turned it slowly and…

The door flew open, propelled by a force from outside.

108.

Alice stumbled backwards, gasping with shock.

Someone was in, a man in black, God, it was him, Archie Jones, but how…?

He was straight at her, a snapshot of his face, twisted with mania, and then she cried out as he began to grapple with her, trying to pin her arms, she yelled again, no one to hear of course, tried to kick him…

'Come on, now, dear, stop it, stop it!' he shouted and then he had a firm grasp of her arms and she tried to knee him in the groin but he twisted sideways, barged his hip into her, she swung her leg back to try and stabilise herself but his attack was so strong, so determined…

She went down underneath him, on to the stairs behind her, and her head hit a step.

109.

'Let's see then, here's the kitchen, what a bloody cheerless, characterless bourgeois room, why don't they ever brighten these places up with a bit of colour, pay some interior designer a couple of monkeys and all they come up with is *slate* greys and *jasmine* whites and *shit* browns…'

She had only been out for a second. When she opened her eyes, lying there against the lower stairs, she could see him through the open door, his back to her, prowling about in the kitchen.

Seven.

That's what she had needed to remember. The policewoman said they'd caught them all, all seven of them.

And there were eight.

So how did Archie escape?

'Oh yes, there we go, that'll have to do as we lost the proper one in the cave, bloody pigs must have nicked it…'

She heard a high metallic zing, a knife being drawn from the block. She slapped a hand over her mouth, too late to stop the gasp of terror.

'Got to make our suit for later, yes indeed, Mister – or should that be Reverend – Clay?'

Archie was talking to himself. Or to…

A strike inside her head, a sharp needle of pain. Alice knew instantly, totally, what had happened in that moment the lights went out in the cave.

The Devil of Tiss had not taken over Ben.

He had possessed Archie.

110.

The pale man turned from the counter and looked back into the hall.

Their eyes met.

'Hi Alice, thought you were out cold,' he said. Then he lifted the broad knife up in front of him. 'Come on now, it won't hurt, not a bit…'

He began to run towards her.

Alice twisted and scrambled up the stairs, slipping and pushing, using her hands, knees and feet, gasping in shock.

Behind her, she heard the clobbering of his Doc Marten boots as he chased her.

'Come on, Alice, such a pretty little face…'

What was he going to do to her?

She was at the top of the stairs, there was a small table and stool by the window. She snatched up the stool, turned and saw him there, below her on the stairs, a desperate gleam in his eyes, his mouth twisted, knife held up, and she struck him, as hard as she could, on the top of the head.

Archie spun and fell down the stairs.

111.

He landed in a foetal curl and didn't move.

Alice stood at the top of the stairs, gasping for breath, watching him.

His eyes were closed. She could see that. He wasn't moving.

Was he dead?

What the hell was going on?

How had he escaped when the police had stormed the cave?

She… she needed to call the police. Now. To get out the house, get to safety. Where was her phone? In the lounge. She noticed her hands were shaking. She had to get past him. Was he dead?

Her vision was blurring with tears.

She didn't want to go down the stairs, to get so close to him. Could she get out the house through a window, escape to her scooter? No, the keys were in the kitchen. She had to go past him. The thought made her sick, in the pit of her stomach.

She… oh God, what was she going to do?

She turned and looked around at the table, the doors to the two bedrooms, the bathroom. She needed something to…

The mirror. She went in the bathroom and picked up the large shaving mirror with its heavy metal stand. Then hurried back to the top of the stairs.

He was still there, in the same position. She could see the knife a good arm's length above his head, near the doormat. Its thick, bright, silver blade.

He must be unconscious.

Tentatively, she took a step down. Watched Archibald Jones. Then another… and another.

There was no sign of him having heard her, no movement at all. She wished there was a cloud of blood blooming above his head, some clear sign he was dead…

She took two more steps down, just three more until she was at the bottom with him…

She studied his face, the large jaw, white, almost anaemic, a little gingerish stubble on his neck and cheek. Pale lashes, closed. He was wearing black tracksuit bottoms, his trucker jacket.

How had he escaped from the cellar? She remembered the candles going out after the police entered, the candelabra pushed over, the fiery shape of Clay pouring into not Ben but Archie, as she now realised…

She had to get past him. Clutching the mirror tightly, she leapt across his prone form and there was a glow, an orange-yellow surrounding her and she…

Felt the searing, hateful, crazed spirit of Horace Clay once again, the Devil of Tiss…

112.

He sits alone in his study, a blank sheet of paper before him.

Trying to write but unable. Because of the Voices. The Voices in his Head.

…He can make Men wonderfully knowing in all the Liberal Sciences… We are Many, we are waiting… He will give you all you need… The Young are your Flesh… He is watching… Build a Shrine on the Rocks… He will come…

'I built the bloody shrine,' he says shrilly, and pushes his pen so hard on the paper he breaks the nib.

…He is a mighty strong Duke…He ruleth Forty Legions…

He looks out the window, up at the moors, the bleak moors, sodden in the rain.

'If I do it, you will bring me back!' he shouts and flings the pen against the window.

…There is always a way back… He will lead you to hidden Treasures… He is a mighty strong Duke… The path to Purification is through Dominion…

'Yes, yes, I know,' he says and clutches his head. Then his hands drop to his sides and he stands. He walks over to the chaise longue and picks up what looks like a treat for a hound, a scrap of ruddy leather gashed with holes. He wraps it slowly across his face, hooks the two stitched straps over his ears. The periphery of the room vanishes as he focuses on the costume made for him by his devoted Acolytes, who came to him from across the land – the outfit that has always given him such pleasure, the tightly fitting tunic and trousers now faded from scarlet to vermillion, the leather tail stiffened with baleen stays that straps around his waist, the heavy gloves stitched with the claws of a bear. Finally, he ties beneath his chin the skull cap adorned with the curled ram's horns.

And feels like… not exactly a God, but certainly one of his Dukes.

He leaves the room and descends into the cellar, the lowest place in the house. There he enters the pentagram, the Sigil of Astaroth, that he has carefully sketched on the brick floor. He thinks about all he has done. About his conviction from an early age, watching with horror his mother beneath the laurel in the clutches of the coachman – those noises she made! – that if God did exist, he was hopeless and unworthy. How he'd kept this belief quiet through his teens and young adulthood so he could obtain a position within the Church – but only so he could learn its weaknesses, plunder the unguarded flanks for esoteric knowledge that would enable him to develop his relationship with the Great Dukes of Hell. A relationship that would open up for him the Path to True Knowledge.

And he had received messages. First from the animals, the sows and rams who had shown him glimpses of the Light when he removed their glistening innards. And then from his Acolytes, those

211

who had urged him to be bold, to make new moves if he wished to have true Dominion over himself and others. So he had captured and sacrificed the women, the first in his cave – seen by the shepherd boy, who fled and fell from the Rocks – and then Carmichael's wife, whose comely face had given him a Vision of the Glory of Astaroth, of a place of Golden Blood and Unutterable Beauty – as well as insight into the Demon's Origins, descended from a Deity of the opposite sex, an ancient, Middle Eastern goddess…

When the locals had finally grown suspicious and gone to the Bishop – he had always known it was just a matter of time – he had decided to make the Final Sacrifice, the leap of Faith that was the ultimate promise to his Lord.

Now here he was, putting shot in his Pistol, preparing for deeper Knowledge, Life Everlasting…

Point the barrel at the head… for He is a mighty Duke and He ruleth Forty Legions…

Forty Legions.

Trust they will bring him back.

And he will have Power over all Manner of Things.

113.

Alice saw all this as she jumped over the body.

Within a few moments of her feet touching the floor she was back to herself, twisting to see if the Devil was still there, if Archie was moving.

But Clay had gone and the man lay still.

So now she knew. Knew why the Reverend so hated women. She snorted. Why were men so fragile when it came to their mothers? And she knew now why he needed a woman's face, to seal his warped communion with the demon he called his master. The male demon with a female provenance…

Her fingers tightened on the mirror and she wondered whether to strike Archie now, on the head, to make sure he was dead. After all, he was a child abductor. And currently possessed by one of the most evil beings Alice had ever come across. Surely if she killed the man Clay would be destroyed too?

She raised the mirror high.

114.

Do it, Alice, he is a Sinner, he deserves to die, do it…

What?

Do it, strike him, he is a Sinner, kill him now before he wakes and kills you, you can kill him, Alice, you have the Power…

She… did. Have the power. She *could* kill him. She looked down at the back of his head, the white skin beneath the fuzz of hair, the outline of the skull.

She could smash that skull with this mirror.

She looked at the mirror in her hand, saw her face, the calm brown eyes, mousy, shoulder-length hair, her mouth slightly open, her crooked incisor…

Do it, Alice, kill Archibald Jones, he is a Bad Man, the path to Purification is through Dominion…

She could do it.

She could kill this evil man.

Kill him, Alice, He is a mighty Duke, He ruleth Forty Legions…

She swung the mirror down.

115.

And smashed it on the ground, beside the prone man's head.

She couldn't do it. She remembered Jo, what happened on the cliffs at Peacehaven. The awful guilt, poor, poor Jo…

No, she wouldn't do it. She couldn't do it.

She was no murderer.

But those voices…

They were just Clay, the residue of his evil chuntering on in her head. Surely?

Snatching up the knife, she ran into the lounge and looked around for her phone. It was there, on the sofa, half tucked beneath a cushion printed with dozens of tiny black cats. She put down the mirror and knife on the couch and unlocked the phone. She backed up slightly as she searched for Inspector Tutt's number, so she could see into the hall through the open doorway.

Archie was getting up!

He was on his hands and knees, shaking his head. As she watched, mouth open in horror, he glanced sideways and their eyes met.

He saw the phone in her hands and suddenly there was a frenzy in him. He began to scramble towards her.

116.

Alice glanced back at her phone, saw the green dial button for Tutt's number, and pushed it, then threw the phone at the man.

He tipped his head to the right, narrowly avoiding it. As he came into the living room, Alice snatched up the knife and moved so the sofa was in between them.

'Careful now, Alice,' said Archie, his hands out in front of him. 'You don't want to be hurting me with that, do you?'

'What do you want?' said Alice.

'Just your face,' he replied. 'Such a lovely face, and Clay needs it, as he said to the boy. So if I can borrow yours, who knows how much it'll help him? I suspect he's struggling to stay here, see…'

'You're mad!' She watched as he swayed a little from side to side, readying himself to spring around the side of the sofa. And she knew, instinctively, she had to keep him talking. Which, given his propensity to rabbit on, might not be too hard – a few pointed questions…

'Who are you people?' she said. 'What do you want?'

'Oh yes, Alice,' said Archie. 'Very good, keep me chatting, I know you're clever. Well, maybe I will talk as, let's face it, one of us isn't going to be leaving here alive.' He grinned, showing those ghastly, oversized teeth. 'We're just a group of ordinary guys and gals who love nature. That's all. But there's more to nature than most people think. There's all the things behind the scenes too. The hidden knowledge – and the hidden beings. The ghosts, they're a part of it, they are nature, too, of course. Quite a few people see them. But then there are other creatures too, older ones. With great understanding. They might be gods, or demons, or just ghosts who have been around for a very long time. No one knows. But with this boy Ben we finally had the chance to find out what it's like over there, on the other side. From Clay. And the one thing any good occultist wants – it's that, above all else. Who knows what might be possible with that fruit, forbidden to all of humanity – so far?'

'Uh-huh,' said Alice, thinking how Aitor had been right all along. 'So it is you speaking now, Archie, and not Clay, isn't it?'

'Yes, it's me, I'm kind of looking after him for the moment. Aren't I, Horace?' He laughed and she saw his eyes briefly unfocus as if he was concentrating on something behind his forehead. Then he said: 'Well, I can't actually hear him, unfortunately. But we both know what he wants, don't we?'

Alice tried not to gasp when she saw the look in his eyes. The lust. Perverse lust. She needed to breathe…

'You're going to need to put the kettle on at this rate, aren't you?' said Archie.

'I can…'

'No, it was a joke, come on, Alice!'

'Vult Scire,' said Alice.

'Vult Scire?' said Archie, looking genuinely surprised. 'You know that name?'

Alice nodded. 'Aitor found something about it. On the web.'

'I've always admired him, very rigorous. A real knack for research. Cuts through all the crap and, as we all know, there's plenty of that to go round in this area.'

'How did the group come to be on the farm?'

'It was Melissa's uncle, she left it to him when he died. She decided to make it into a base for the group, because it's close to the Rocks. And, because she worked for the Water Company and they needed to do some conservation on the moors as part of their contract – their *corporate social responsibility*, as they call it – they got themselves set up as a charity that could do the work. An

216

incredible opportunity to be near this place of power. You must have felt it, Alice, surely?'

She gave a small nod.

'Beautiful place, the Rocks. Throbbing with inner life. Kind of… calls… to special people all over the world. Which is where the Frenchwoman came in.'

'Who?'

'Bee…something.'

Alice was thinking. Keep him talking. *Bee* sounded familiar, where…?

'Anyway, she's the one who built a relationship with the boy. And, sick of his disbelieving old grandpa, he shared something with her. His big secret.'

'He could talk to ghosts.'

It was Archie's turn to nod, beaming. 'She had to leave after he told her, go back home because there was something up, but when she let them at the farm know about the boy they couldn't believe their luck. This was their chance – the first chance in human history! – to find out what was beyond the veil. Do you see, Alice – I can see you do, yes!'

'They realised they needed to get the ghost and boy in the same place at once. They decided to try and summon him first in his old home, where he made his pact with the Dukes.'

'Of Hazzard?' said Alice.

'Of Hell,' said Archie. She had expected him to chuckle, but he was serious. 'They wanted to check they could do it, before they tried it out in earnest on the Rocks with the boy.'

'And it worked, of course.'

'Yes. They did it a few months ago and it all went to plan. Sneaked into the house, they did – people are so careless about security these days – and brought him back whilst the old vicar slept upstairs and the boy was at school!'

'So why did you come?'

'They called me in because I'm a psychometrist.'

'A what?' said Alice.

'A psychometrist. I can tell the history of objects, things about their owners, just by holding them.'

Alice shuddered, remembering the creepy way he'd held her arm when she was showing him the directions to the farm on his phone.

'So that's why they wanted the boy's toy sheep?' she said.

'Exactly, you are a smart girl, Alice. I used it to confirm what they already suspected, that he was a sensitive. And not just any old sensitive, an extraordinary one! One who could *actually talk* to the buggers!'

'So… how did you escape when the police came in?'

Archie smiled. 'I found the small tunnel at the back the day before, when I was checking out the cave. All I needed to do was get the lights out.'

Alice nodded, remembering falling to her knees after her dreadful vision, seeing the passage at the back of the cave.

'And Douglas – was it you who you killed him?'

'The old priest? No, after Blake and Mel captured the boy, they went back to the house. Planning to, err, put him out of our misery, as we couldn't risk him sounding the alarm when he found his grandson gone. But very strange, they found he was dead already.'

Alice shook her head slowly.

'Maybe he'd been visited by Horace again?' said Archie. 'One final time, which polished him off.'

'You're…'

'What, Alice? What are we?' Archie studied her intently, a wry grin on his face. 'We're Vult Scire. People who want to know…'

When she said nothing, he stopped swaying and looked down at the shagpile rug he was standing on. 'Anyways, Alice, you got me talking long enough.' He looked up at her. 'You've got something we need now.'

He pointed at her face, waggled the knife, then dived across the sofa and collided with her…

117.

Roughly, he drags her into the cave, one hand holding her long hair, the other around her throat.

She struggles against him, screaming all the way, digging her nails into his arms, pushing her calves against the gritty rock, feet slipping sideways, trying all she can…

A gasp.

'Be still, you harlot,' he says, shaking her hard, pulling her further into the darkness that soon grows light again, not with natural sunlight but the illumination of dozens of candles in the walls of the stone chamber. Dimly, she is aware there are others here, robed, shaven-headed figures in the background. And then she is made more forcibly aware of them as one helps the wicked Reverend pin her down and another hands him… a knife.

'Aah!' a voice hisses in her ear.

'No!' she screams as his hand, big and brutish, shoves her head to one side and holds it down despite all her efforts. The other man is holding her shoulder and someone else has kneeled across her legs. She sees a solitary candle, a high nib of unmelted wax beside the flame, on a dish set in the niche near her eyes.

In her peripheral vision she sees him bring the ancient-looking knife, its broad flat blade, up to her cheek.

'Now…' he says.

'Oh God,' says a man.

As the knife gouges the side of her face and blood spills, he feels a thrill of energy, some wild connection made…

'Oh yes, Alice, that's good…'

And then out from the pinned woman a double rises, a pale shape of the woman whose face is being cut, but she is no longer in a memory – or rather no longer in the Reverend's memory – and the ghost's face is whole, not damaged, and in the sequence like a dream the brutish Clay sees her and Alice realises it is no longer the historical Clay but rather the spirit in the man above her – the gasping man, Archie Jones – and the ghost of Gretel is reaching up and taking the Devil's throat in her hands, feeling round the strap that holds on that stupid skull cap with its ridiculous horns and, instead of helping, the Acolytes are standing back and they are starting to speak things, they are saying, He is a Mighty Duke, He ruleth Forty Legions, He makes Men wonderfully knowing in the Liberal Sciences, the path to Purification is through Dominion…

'Harder, Alice, yes, you have form with this. I can see now, something about a guy in… Wales… did you… what did you…?'

And they chant as the spirit of Clay in Archibald Jones panics, tries to push the vengeful ghost-woman away – the wife of that oaf Carmichael who barely speaks the Queen's English – but he can't and she continues to crush his windpipe with her thumbs, now he's vulnerable in this critically injured host, and his breath won't come, he feels the constriction building in his body, an empty striving in his chest, her fierce grey eyes blazing into his, his body shaking with desperation, his lungs immobile, needing air, but there is none, no more, and as the female spectre grips him mercilessly by the neck and shows absolute satisfaction in her expression he feels frenzied terror because if he leaves now, in this scenario that should be imaginary but isn't, what will happen to him, will he no longer be a promised Leader of the Legions, will he go somewhere he doesn't know, will he go anywhere at all or will it be the…?

And he is gone.

118.

She blinked, feeling a wetness on her cheek.

She smelt a stench, like a rotten carcass, and wanted to look away from the face, the large open jaw, just above her.

Archie Jones. Eyes closed. Pinning her down, drooling on her.

A dead weight.

Alice gasped and used all her strength to wrestle him off her, twisting sideways from beneath him. As she did so, she felt the knife she'd been holding twist and jar awkwardly in her hand. She let it go, rolled away, feeling a slickness on her hand and wrist.

Blood. Archie's blood.

'Oh no…' she said. She pushed him over on his back and the kitchen knife, already loosened by her movement, slipped easily out from his midriff, blood oozing around it.

She stood and ran out into the hall, then snatched her phone up from the floor. She unlocked the splintered screen and saw that the call to Inspector Tutt was live, still in progress.

'Hello!' she said.

'Alice?' said the Inspector. 'Alice – are you…'

'I think I've killed him,' she said.

119.

'There's a car on its way, Alice,' said the Inspector. 'Don't panic. When the call connected, I could hear it all, everything that was said. Do you need to get out the house?'

'I – I probably should,' said Alice. 'Or should I… perhaps I should do first aid?'

'What happened?'

'He broke into the house – Archie Jones, one of *them* – and tried to attack me with a knife. But I… I stabbed him.'

'Stay calm, Alice. The car won't be long.'

'OK,' she said, glancing around fitfully. In the living room, she couldn't see Archie anymore because he was behind the door. She was getting that feeling, the one where the light was growing in intensity and it felt like she was being crowded out of her own head. Panic. At least she knew it now, understood the feeling better…

She should get her scooter keys, ride down to the village. If she left the door open, the police and emergency services could get in…

'I'm going to leave now,' she said and then, when the Inspector didn't reply, she realised she had accidentally cut him off.

Should she dial him back again… or flee?

She decided to get out. She turned towards the kitchen and then caught sight of a movement to her right in… the living room.

She spun round in terror, expecting to see Archie standing there.

But instead saw *her*.

Gretel Carmichael.

The Grackle.

120.

She was standing by the window, a pale fuzz of human form in dull afternoon light.

Alice could see her white, shapeless dress, long dark hair – the terrible scraps of flesh, the exposed slivers of bone on her face. Which no longer frightened her, but instead filled her with intense pity.

The ghost began to come towards her. Ethereal, drifty, adrift. This time Alice didn't back away, even when she came right up to her and she could see in detail the horror of her face, the places where patches of red skin and white underflesh were still attached to the yellowish skull. The stark warning of those long, gumless teeth. The pink flesh that remained in the hollows of the eye sockets.

Did not back away as the ghost took hold of her.

121

She is looking down at him as he sleeps and feeling it all.

The hatred. The all-consuming hatred for them. *For all those men of the cloth, with their quiet perversions, their evil acts, their murders – but most of all, with their unconscionable hypocrisy, the way they hold themselves up as leaders to the masses. The pure, the seers, those who know how to behave and can tell us what we are to do.*

This old man, this old man of the cloth, she hates him.

HATES HIM.

He coughs, his lungs straining as they sustain the last morsels of life in his piteous body. Dimly, she is aware of his connection to the precious one, the boy she loves and cares for, who sleeps in the same house. But… only dimly, and with no regard for it.

She will keep the boy safe from Clay and his wicked disciples. And she will do it much better than this pathetic soul.

The old man coughs again.

And then he opens his eyes, pale and quickly seeing in the dark, seeing the horror above him.

And as he sees she lunges at him, screaming silently, showing him the wreck of her being, her shocking face, her grey teeth, the back of her black throat, shaking her dark hair at him, the full force of her malice striking him like a hammer between the eyes, knocking its violent charge right down into the core of his feeble heart…

122.

'Douglas...'

Alone now, Alice stood by the window, staring at the place where the ghost had been.

Silence.

She was gone.

Alice turned, took one horrified glance at the sprawling form of Archibald Jones, then ran from her house.

A Meeting in the Park

123.

'Alice!'

She had not known what to expect when she went in the ward, clutching the book. But as soon as she saw him there, propped up on pillows, sucking drink through a straw, her heart leapt with happiness.

'Aitor!'

She hurried to his side, passing three empty beds on the way. The ward was clear except for two old women at the far end.

She stopped, examining his sling, the heavily bandaged shoulder. 'Can we hug?'

'Sure, Alice,' he said, setting down his drink carton and spreading his right arm. She hugged him carefully, avoiding his injured side, feeling a mixture of anxiety and joy.

She drew back and sat down in the plastic chair beside him.

'Got you this,' she said, showing him the cover of the book. It was a history of the Aztecs, something she knew he'd like. 'Have you read it?'

'No, not that one,' he said. 'Perfect!'

She beamed at him, then looked again at the bandage. 'How is it now?' she said.

'Still a bit painful, to be honest,' he replied.

'But it'll get better…?'

'Of course. Luckily our friend with the chopper missed the main arteries in my neck. The blade went in at the shoulder, was stopped when it smashed my collar bone. But…' he lifted his injured arm a little and showed her his fingers, '…he managed to do damage to one of my nerves, so I'm having trouble waggling these…'

She saw his thumb, index and little fingers close, but the middle and ring fingers barely moved.

'Oh, Aitor…' she said, putting a hand on his shin through the blanket.

'Let's see how it goes,' he said. 'One little Basque is just very – *very* – grateful to be alive.'

'Did you see your mum?'

'Yes, of course. She came up on her motorbike. Told me I was a naughty boy, going in when we should have waited for the police.'

'Oh, I feel awful…' Alice began.

'No! Then she said I didn't do anything she wouldn't have done.' He grinned, then his face dropped and he said quickly: 'Tell me, how are you? The Inspector told me much of it, but I can't believe what you had to go through – again…'

'I'm OK,' said Alice. 'But… all those interviews with the police, Aitor, and… and the funeral of Douglas…

Aitor sighed. 'I wish I could have been there.'

Alice looked at him and said: 'And Aitor… Archie's still alive.'

'I thought he was going to die.'

'He's still in a coma.'

'He may as well stay in it,' said Aitor. 'He'll only be going to prison when he comes out of it. For the rest of his life.'

Alice nodded. 'Yes, I know,' she said. 'Or at least, for a very long time. He didn't actually kill anyone. Only attempted to. Thankfully, Inspector Tutt heard a lot of incriminating things on the phone.'

'That'll make things a lot easier,' said Aitor. Then he laughed and said: 'I bet a lot of it must have utterly confused the poor man!'

Alice shrugged. 'I'm sure,' she said.

Aitor looked at her. 'At least the phone evidence – alongside everything else – means there won't be any charges?' he said.

She could hear the uncertainty in his voice. 'Hopefully,' she said. 'DI Tutt has liaised with the CPS. He says it's a clearcut case of self-defence.'

'You'll be alright, Alice,' said Aitor, squeezing her hand. 'And what about the others?'

'It's going to be a long time before it all comes out,' said Alice. 'They're all either child kidnappers or accessories, so they'll be going down.'

'Crazies,' said Aitor. 'Absolute bloody nutters…'

Alice nodded.

Aitor gazed at her. 'Have you seen her again since Archie attacked you? Gretel?'

'No. But I've been thinking about her. Especially that last moment when I saw what she'd done to Douglas. Or rather, when she showed me what she'd done to him.'

'Yes, I was shocked,' said Aitor. 'I thought it must have been Clay who killed him – or just his illness, finally taking its toll.'

'I was stunned too,' said Alice. 'It was horrific, poor Douglas. And it was strange too, for another reason…'

'What's that?'

'Normally when I merge with spirits, I only see the thing they're hinged around, a grief or anger relating to an injustice, or at least something intense from when they were alive – like Clay and his murders. But in this case, she showed me something she'd done *as a ghost*.'

'That is fascinating,' said Aitor. 'It underlines the agency of ghosts even further. Another one for us to mull over when we get a bit of distance from all this…' He stroked his lip for a moment, thinking, then said: 'Why do you think she did it?'

'Guilt. I think she was dimly aware of the relationship between the boy and his grandad, his last living relative. She must have known, no matter how bad her own experience had been, that all priests weren't bad. And she took him away from Ben.'

'How awful,' said Aitor. 'But it makes sense. I assume you're not going to tell Ben about it?'

Alice shook her head. 'I couldn't,' she said.

A nurse appeared with a menu. 'What would you like for lunch, Aitor?' she said. She had a lovely smile, broad and generous and Alice noticed her eyes twinkling.

'What's the hot meal, Nerys?' he asked, tilting his head to look at the menu.

'Cottage pie,' she said. 'Again.'

'I'd better have the salad,' he said, with a grin.

'OK.' She spun around and walked off towards the old women.

'Bad food?' said Alice.

Aitor gritted his teeth and winced. 'Darling, you wouldn't believe what they do to food in this place.'

'It's all microwaved, I guess,' she said.

'Even the salad,' he said and they laughed. Then he said: 'You're learning so much about the afterlife…'

She glanced out of the window at the bleak sky and said: 'Aitor – you know what really frightens me?'

'No,' he said quietly.

She was surprised by a surge of feeling, which made her afraid she might cry. She pinched her nose, then said: 'It's not *seeing* them, Aitor. Nor even feeling their feelings. It's… it's the terror of the… well…' she took a deep breath. 'We know they are real, you and me. So how do we know…'

Aitor reached out and held her wrist.

'How do we know, Aitor, when we die, we won't *become* one of them?'

He looked at her.

'How do we know we won't become ghosts?' she said. 'What would it be like, trapped for eternity in a half-world, with undying pain? The Unhome, as Clay called it. That for me would be hell, Aitor. It's hell.'

Aitor leaned forward and she let him put his good arm around her, ignoring the slight wince she heard. She remembered seeing red, holding that mirror high and hearing that voice in her head, her desire to crack Archie's head open. Surely she would never…?

She needed to be held.

'One day at a time, Alice,' he said quietly in her ear. 'You're thinking about what happened to Clay, because he lived the life he led. For whatever reason – because of something he did, intentionally or unintentionally, or because of some hidden karma – he didn't cross over. He stayed in a hellish place that might have been of his own making. I suspect the place that your Reading Man – or even the woman I saw in Guernica, searching for her son – might be very different. Hard perhaps, but not so tortuous. And then there is always the hope that a wrong will be righted, that you can cross over to the other side. Which, I strongly suspect, is a place of peace.'

'But who knows, Aitor?' Alice bit her thumbnail.

'No one,' he said. 'Anything could happen in the future. But what we do know is ourselves, now. We go forwards from here.'

When she drew back, she felt the tearfulness had passed. 'You really are good to me,' she said.

He smiled. 'Do you know what I'm scared about?' he said.

She shook her head.

'Forget ghosts – it's people! Especially the kind we've come into contact with recently. Do you know how scared I was when that light went on at the farm? Darling, I would never leave you, you know that, but it took every last bit of Aitor's courage for him to come back and find you!'

She laughed, shaking her head. 'Yes,' she said. 'People are scary, too.'

'Have you seen Ben since the funeral?' he said.

'I'm seeing him tomorrow,' she said. 'He's asked for me…'

124.

He was standing in the bandstand, a woman in a scarf beside him.

The appalling weather had continued through November but today was a rare day of sunshine, bright clouds rearranging themselves in the sky. Most trees had given up their leaves already, but a few coppery husks were still drifting down from the oaks as Alice crossed the park and climbed the steps into the bandstand.

Ben ran up and threw his arms around her. She hugged him back, looking awkwardly at the woman.

'Mrs Freeman?' she said, still holding him. She smiled as she spotted Sheepy, scruffy and eternally kind, watching over the top of his backpack.

'Yes. I guess I don't need to check that you're Alice,' said the woman kindly. She was middle-aged, maybe in her mid-fifties, with high cheekbones and an appearance of glamour and good health that reminded Alice of some American actress.

'Would you like a few minutes alone?' asked the woman.

Alice and Ben released each other, and she smiled at him. He turned and looked back at Mrs Freeman and nodded.

'I'll go to the pavilion and get a coffee,' she said.

125.

'How are you?'

'Fine.'

'You're happy with that lady?'

'Yes.' Ben watched Mrs Freeman as she headed across the park to the pavilion. 'Her and her husband William are amazing,' he said. 'They look after so many kids. There are two more with them now and one of them, his name's Vasil, he's from Bulgaria, his dad was killed by accident in a fight between gangs. His family wasn't involved at all, but someone thought his dad was

Romanian. And his dad was his only relative, so they had to take him into care, like me…'

He looked down, touched his shoes together. Alice felt her heart melt. Again.

'I'm so sorry about your grandad, Ben,' she said. 'He was a wonderful man. He told me that night we were together how highly he thought of you. And how he wished he'd told you more often.'

He continued to look down. 'Thanks,' he said quietly.

'I'm here for you,' she said. 'Anytime you need me, day or night. You have my number.'

He nodded.

'Has she – the Grackle – been back to you?'

'No.'

Alice swept a strand of hair back that had blown into her eyes. 'You and me, we both have a special gift,' she said, wishing she had rehearsed what she wanted to say to him. 'We can see ghosts… and we can help them too. The ones who deserve helping. And you – you can speak with them too. That's… amazing.'

'I want to be normal,' he said.

'I understand that,' she said. 'I do too. But, for some reason, we haven't been given that choice. Who knows why, the world is one big mystery. But maybe one day, your gift will change something important in our unfathomable world.'

She looked at him, uncertain whether what she was saying would make him feel better or worse. She remembered one of her mum's friends, a retired counsellor, giving her advice when she was an anxious teenager that was exactly the opposite of what she wanted to hear, all about the *precious individuality of her experience*. All she'd wanted was to know her feelings were normal, something everyone went through.

When he looked up at her with an open expression, she realised she was being too self-critical. He needed the reassurance.

'There is one thing I wanted to ask you though, Ben,' she said, drawing in a deep breath. 'One piece of the puzzle I haven't fully worked out.'

He tipped his head down, in a way she thought meant her to go on.

'Those people – the awful cult people – they somehow knew you had the ability to speak to ghosts. Do you know how they might have found out? One of them talked about a French lady. Was she the one who came to speak to your grandad?'

For a moment, Alice couldn't remember her name, so much had happened in the last few weeks. Then it came back. *Bee-something*, Archie had called her…

'Brielle?' she said.

Ben nodded.

'Why… why did you tell her?' Alice couldn't imagine.

'She used to meet me in the village on my way home from school. Most days, she would buy me a drink and a slice of cake in the pub café. She was nice.'

'So you told her about this thing you could do?'

'Yes. She told me about all the ghosts she had found and I told her about the Grackle and how we spoke to each other.'

'And how did she… how did she react?'

'She wanted to know more. She was quite… excited, I suppose. Keen. She said she knew it was probably scary but one day I'd realise how special my power – she called it a power – was.'

So there was a connection between this French woman and Vult Scire, as Archie had indicated. Who was she? Maybe she would never know…

Alice saw the boy was looking at her searchingly now, as if he wanted her to tell him her thoughts.

'My friend Aitor showed me how the cult members might have found out about you, on the web,' she said. 'I think maybe she put something on one of the forums they used. That's probably how they knew.'

He accepted it with a small nod. And then, as children do, his expression changed and he looked doubtfully at her.

'I might not be with this family long,' he said. 'They just take emergency cases. So… I'd really like to stay friends with you… if that's alright?'

She nodded vigorously.

'I'll always be your friend, Ben,' she said and held him tight again, as if he was her own child.

Thank you for reading my book, I hope you enjoyed it!

If you did I would be very grateful if you could post a rating or write a short review on Amazon or Goodreads. Your ratings make a real difference to authors, helping the books you enjoy reach more people.

The Ghosts of Alice

The Ghosts of Alice is a new series of standalone ghost stories featuring Alice Deaton, a young woman with a mysterious connection with the dead.

The Boy in the Burgundy Hood

**** THE #1 INTERNATIONAL BESTSELLER ****

Will it be her dream job – or a waking nightmare?

Alice can't believe her luck when she lands a new post at a medieval English manor house. Mired in debt, the elderly owners have transferred their beloved Bramley to a heritage trust. Alice must prepare it for opening to the public, with the former owners relegated to a private wing.

But when the ghosts start appearing - the woman with the wounded hand and the boy in the burgundy hood - Alice realises why her predecessor might have left the isolated house so soon.

As she peels back the layers of the mystery, the secrets Alice uncovers haunting Bramley's heart will be dark - darker than she could ever have imagined…

The Girl in the Ivory Dress

Will a strange request help her move on from a haunted past?

After a fire tears through the country house where she works, Alice accepts a desperate invitation from a friend whose guest house is being haunted.

But when Alice arrives at Peacehaven, she senses something much stranger going on. Who is the ghastly spectre roaming the house? Why is he terrifying the guests? And why does Alice keep dreaming about the ghosts of her past, the burning man and girl in the ivory dress?

As she digs deeper, Alice will uncover an insidious evil that might just overwhelm her...

About the Author

Steve Griffin writes chilling ghost stories for adults and thrilling adventure stories for teens.

He finds inspiration anywhere and everywhere. An interview his wife had for a job in a remote country manor inspired the bestselling *The Boy in the Burgundy Hood*. His travels around India, Africa and America – combined with the discovery of a stunning garden deep in the English countryside – led to the portal mystery series, *The Secret of the Tirthas*. The first book of the series, *The City of Light*, was described in *The Guardian* as 'entertaining and exciting.'

Steve lives in the Surrey Hills with his wife and two sons. He loves walking, watching horror movies and going to indie gigs.

For news of his writing, sign up to his newsletter by emailing stevegriffin.author@outlook.com, or subscribe at steve-griffin.com.

You can also connect with him via @stevegriffin.author on Instagram and Facebook.

Printed in Great Britain
by Amazon